MATEO

The K9 Files

Dale Mayer

MATEO: THE K9 FILES, BOOK 30
Beverly Dale Mayer
Valley Publishing Ltd.

ISBN-13: 978-1-778866-91-3
Print Edition

Books in This Series:

Ethan, Book 1

Pierce, Book 2

Zane, Book 3

Blaze, Book 4

Lucas, Book 5

Parker, Book 6

Carter, Book 7

Weston, Book 8

Greyson, Book 9

Rowan, Book 10

Caleb, Book 11

Kurt, Book 12

Tucker, Book 13

Harley, Book 14

Kyron, Book 15

Jenner, Book 16

Rhys, Book 17

Landon, Book 18

Harper, Book 19

Kascius, Book 20

Declan, Book 21

Bauer, Book 22

Delta, Book 23

Conall, Book 24

Baron, Book 25

Walton, Book 26

Cage, Book 27

Trey, Book 28

Austin, Book 29

Mateo, Book 30

Wilden, Book 31

Boxed Sets and Bundles

https://geni.us/Bundlepage

About This Book

Welcome to the all new K9 Files series reconnecting readers with the unforgettable men from SEALs of Steel in a new series of action packed, page turning romantic suspense that fans have come to expect from USA TODAY Bestselling author Dale Mayer. Pssst… you'll meet other favorite characters from SEALs of Honor and Heroes for Hire too!

Mateo is always ready to help, especially when it comes to animals. When Kat, her War Dog files in hand, suggests he find out what happened to Thorny, the latest missing K9 dog, Mateo eagerly agrees. But it's not just the dog that's missing—the entire family has vanished, and the reasons are unexpectedly complex.

Maraya, with a heart full of concern, has been trying to get anyone to care about the missing family next door. Her tarnished reputation in town makes it difficult, and a welfare check leads nowhere when no one answers the door.

Thorny is eventually found in the woods, fiercely guarding a small boy from the missing family. This discovery sparks interest—but not in a good way. As Mateo and Maraya delve deeper, they uncover hidden secrets and a budding romance, adding layers of intrigue to their quest.

Sign up to be notified of all Dale's releases here!
https://geni.us/DaleNews

K AT STARED AT Badger, a big grin on her face. "It really worked," she crowed.

He just shook his head. "I can't believe it, and Rox actually called you?"

"I knew about Austin, and she knew about Austin, so you know about stubbornness. Sometimes you just have to try to get people to do something that maybe they didn't think they should do," she explained, followed by a laugh, "but I am thrilled."

"So am I." Badger shook his head. "Just amazing. So is there only one more?"

"Only one, at least for the moment," she clarified, as she looked at the file in front of them.

Badger asked, "You've got Mateo for this one?

"I do, and I've asked him about it, but I haven't really told him what it is."

"Of course not, but you may want to give him a heads-up though."

"He told me that he's ready for anything. He just needs to get out and to find something else to do with his life. So, I thought this might be a good one for him."

"Maybe, maybe it is. Where is it?"

"In Virginia," she replied. "I don't even have very much. I just have the adopted family and a note saying that a wellness check didn't show any signs of anybody being there."

"So, we don't know what happened?"

"I followed up with the local police, and all they had was that the entire family has gone missing."

"The entire family?"

"Yeah." Kat nodded, looking at Badger worriedly. "As in, from one day to the next, nobody has seen them. The vehicle is still there but nothing else."

"Murdered?"

"We don't know, but …"

"What about anybody else? Anybody got anything?"

Kat sighed. "One of the neighbors mentioned a young woman had come and gone a couple times, trying to raise some attention to the case, but I'm not sure that anybody was necessarily looking into it to her satisfaction. So I'll put Mateo in touch with her, and we'll see if we can get this one solved too."

"I would hate to think the last one would beat us," Badger muttered.

"It won't," Kat declared.

Badger walked closer and wrapped his arms around her. "I have faith in you."

She smiled up at her husband. "That could be misplaced faith."

"It could be, but, even if so, it's still good."

"We have done something … really phenomenal."

He stopped, then laughed. "No, *you* have done something phenomenal. So, trust in that and rejoice. We'll see this one through and then see what happens. So far you haven't been wrong yet."

She grinned at him, a twinkle in her eye. "Let's hope I'm not this time either."

CHAPTER 1

Mateo Montgomery stepped out of his truck, closed the door, and turned to look around. It was another hot sunny day, which was just a continuation of every other day in Virginia, even in this small town of Culpeper. He pulled his sweaty T-shirt away from his chest and back, flapping the shirt to give his body a little bit of fresh air, as he considered the rundown house in front of him.

It wasn't what he expected. Somebody who had adopted a War Dog would normally have gone through a screening process to ensure they were prepared for the expense and the cost of caring for a dog like this. However, the house in front of Mateo had seen far better days and needed rescuing itself.

He frowned as he stepped forward and walked up the front steps, double-checking the address on his phone as he went. It was definitely the right place, and that was even more disturbing. He wasn't into judging people, but he also recognized that, when people experienced times of struggle, their pets sometimes suffered the most. Children too, but that wasn't the focus here. Up at the front door, he stopped and knocked. His heavy knock swung the door slowly open.

Swearing at that, he stepped inside and called out, "Hello? Anyone here? … Hello?"

He got no answer, and, given the ramshackle look of the

place, that was not too surprising. Still, he hoped for a little more knowledge of what was going on here. He walked through the main floor of the house, noting it was still furnished, but everything was very old, very worn, of very little value, except—for those who had so little—just something to sit on.

He meandered through the house, going upstairs to check out the bedrooms. It was a small abode, with three bedrooms, one of which looked completely uninhabited, or at least hadn't been used for sleeping. As he made his way into what should have been the master bedroom, he found clothes everywhere, as if the residents had taken off on short notice, maybe planning to come back for whatever else they needed.

Either way, it wasn't a good look.

As he stood here and stared, a woman called out from downstairs, "Hello?"

He immediately retraced his steps to the hallway, looked down the stairwell, and saw a young woman with bright red curly hair, flying in every direction, her chest heaving as if she had run for miles. "Hey," he replied. "Do you know where the family is?"

Her gaze flew upward, as she frowned at him. "I was hoping you were the family," she stated abruptly.

He shook his head. "I'm here for the dog that they have."

Her eyebrows shot up. "Dog?" she repeated.

He nodded. "The family had adopted a War Dog," he explained, as he walked down the stairs, taking it a little easy on his back. For every step he felt a wave of pain hit his back, as if slamming him against a sharp rock, then slowly ebbing away.

She shook her head, then spoke. "Are you talking about Thorny?"

He shrugged. "I have him listed as Blake, but it's not uncommon for people to change the name. This dog is more shepherd-looking than Malinois, his coloring a little bit darker than normal for a shepherd."

She nodded. "Yes, that's him."

"Have you seen him?" She hesitated, and he narrowed his gaze at her. "I am here on behalf of the War Department," he added, hoping that would be enough to shake her tongue loose.

She flushed, then nodded. "Yes, in a way I know where he is, kind of. He was with the family, but now I don't know where the family is," she shared in frustration. "And you probably already know this, but that is a damn good dog."

"Absolutely," he murmured, trying to figure out what was going on here. He studied her as he slowly made his way to the landing and then down the last few steps. "Do you know when the family left?"

"I don't even know that they left, at least not voluntarily. I've been trying to get people to look into it, but nobody cares," she complained.

"How many people lived here?"

She looked at him strangely and noted, "For someone sent by the War Department, you don't seem to have a whole lot of information on them."

"I want to confirm that it's the same family," he stated.

She brushed back her hair, sending unruly curls into a wild flutter around her face.

"I need some confirmation."

"Two kids, with their mother and father," she told him, "but I'm worried about the kids. ... Emily too, but a part of me—No, no, I don't need to say that."

"Anything you can tell me would be a help," he pointed out. "I gather you're quite worried about them."

She nodded. "I've known the family for quite a while, yet in many ways I don't know anything about them."

"You want to explain that?"

She groaned. "Nothing to be found here. You can come back to my place if you want, and I'll tell you the little bit I do know."

He nodded. "And just where is your place?" he asked.

"I'm right next door," she said, resignation in her tone.

He could see a property nearby. Not close enough to see the house, but close enough that he could see the rooftop.

"I'm Maraya Banks."

"Mateo Montgomery. And did you see me arrive?" he asked, as they walked toward her house. "Because you sure arrived fast."

"I feel as if I have eyes in the back of my head when it comes to this place right now. I keep hoping that they will show up soon." She chewed on her bottom lip.

He studied her closely. "You obviously have fears, and the police may not believe that your fears are warranted, but you can't seem to get it out of your mind. I can understand that. So maybe you could fill me in as to what exactly you think is going on."

"I don't know," she muttered, then groaned. "Maybe it's just me, and I'm making too much out of it."

"You have to tell me what you know," he pointed out, "so maybe somebody could help you."

"I would love it if somebody would help me," she snapped and took a deep breath, "but, honest to God, the world is a little short on help."

He nodded. "Sometimes, but not always."

"You came here to look for a dog," she replied, shaking her head, "and I know a hell of a lot of people are out there who could use a hand. No offense intended, but *people* need help. They sure won't get it from any law enforcement department because they're homeless *illegal aliens*, as they call them," she muttered in a mocking tone, "or any other number of issues dealing with mental health, drug addictions, and related things."

"I'm not here to argue about the social mess that we're in at the moment," he said, trying to keep his tone neutral, "but believe me that this family concerns me right now."

She stepped up onto her front porch, and he took note of her really nice beach-style home that was obviously lovingly maintained. "This is a beautiful house," he said, with a smile. "Have you lived here long?"

"All my life," she replied. "It was the family home, and my father put a lot of time and effort into keeping it beautiful."

"And he did a hell of a job," he agreed, as he admired the huge wraparound porch. "Nothing quite like a porch such as this to speak volumes about a home."

She smiled, looking out to her small front yard. "And that's how I look at it. Not everybody else does though."

"Of course not," he murmured. He looked at the two big old chairs on the front porch and asked, "May I?"

She nodded immediately. "Yes, please do. I may calm down a bit myself if I sat and relaxed a little too." She added, "I was very disappointed that you weren't them."

"How well do you know them?"

"I know the kids pretty well," she shared. "I was teaching here locally up until a bit ago, and they were part of my classrooms."

"Ah, that's good." He smiled. "So, in that case, you should know something about them."

"You would think so," she muttered in a wry tone. "Yet the fact that I was a local and living here didn't seem to make them any friendlier. … Even that sounds wrong because it's not as if they were unfriendly. I think they were just loners in a way. Yet one other thing makes them sound really bad. And I don't quite know how to explain it."

"The best way is to just come right out with it," he suggested. "Particularly if you know something."

"It's not that I know something," she clarified, raising her hands. "However, I know something about the family."

"I would appreciate any details you can give me."

"Okay. Apparently the husband came back from the military, after doing a couple tours, and he wasn't the same."

Mateo's heart sank as he heard that news, but he slowly nodded. "It happens. … It's quite an adjustment for soldiers when they come home."

"Sure it is," she stated, her expression of distaste clear. "I don't dispute that, believe me. I've seen the news, and I can't imagine what the military goes through. Yet this was his family, and I know that things were getting … intense, and the family was afraid of him."

"In what way?" he asked, trying to keep his tone neutral.

"He was explosive, more violent, getting paranoid about everything. He didn't want the children in school anymore, wanted his wife to homeschool them, things like that."

"Why?"

"He thought that they were being watched and that people were coming after him. Therefore, they would also be coming after his family."

Mateo settled back and studied her for a long moment. "Okay, in some ways that makes an unfortunate amount of sense."

"I know, right?" she noted. "Yet when I tried to tell anybody that I think either he's done something to the family or he's taken them away, potentially against their will, nobody—and I mean, not a single person—would talk to me."

"Because there's no proof, right?"

"No proof except for the fact that the house is empty, where two kids, a wife, and a husband used to be," she declared. "Apparently that's not enough evidence."

"It's not enough evidence for them to immediately blame the father," he pointed out, "but it is enough of a concern that the local authorities should be checking into these missing people."

"Yeah, well, they say they did and found nothing to support a claim of violence or abuse."

"And you don't believe them?"

She winced. "I—It's not that I don't believe them," she replied carefully. "It just seems to me that a bare minimum effort was put into checking it out."

"And why is that?"

She shrugged. "I don't want to jump to the obvious, which is the fact that the missing family is Mexican-born but US citizens, and it does seem that maybe they were not given the same attention that other people might have gotten."

"You mean, white people."

"And I don't even want to say that," she said sharply, "because I don't know that to be true. I just feel as if I can't get anybody to care, and it concerns me."

"Of course," he noted, "particularly if you know the kids."

"I do know the kids, and I did argue with Carlos about getting them back into the classroom, but he wasn't having it. As far as he was concerned, no good could come from their going there. Timmy and Donna are good kids."

"*No good for them*? How do you figure? Were they in any danger?"

She pondered that for a long moment. "I'm not exactly sure. Once Carlos got something in his head, it was almost impossible to change his mind or his focus on it."

"That may be, and sometimes the rationale isn't always clear," he shared, "but, from my experience, some rationale should always be behind everything we do. It might be misguided, or even just plain wrong, but usually something is behind it."

"All I heard from Emily was that Carlos had gotten very strange, had gotten quite … she didn't say *violent*. She didn't say *abusive*, but I got the impression that she was scared."

"Scared of Carlos?"

"Yes, I got that impression."

"And yet she stayed. Why?"

"Because she loved him, because he was the father of her children, because he came back from the war damaged," she explained, "like so many other veterans. It wasn't his fault, and he needed help and support, but"—she took a breath—"I also understand that he refused to reach out and get any of that."

"Which is the next problem," he murmured.

"Exactly," she agreed.

"It's hard to force anybody to get help unless they really want it, and many of them don't."

"You seem to know all about it."

"Yeah, I do," he declared, turning his gaze back to her.

"I spent ten years in the navy myself."

She nodded. "Then you're one of the lucky ones, if you came back whole."

He paused for half a beat. "I don't think any of us ever quite come back *whole*," he clarified, with a dry laugh. "Yet we try to find ways to cope and to adjust to the new reality of the world we've returned to."

She stared at him and then smiled. "Sounds as if you are in better shape than some I've seen."

"And that is quite possible," he acknowledged, shooting her a knowing smile. "Now, is there any chance this family just went back to Mexico?"

"I don't know," she shared. "Emily told me that Carlos would never return because he didn't have any support there. He apparently wasn't at all close to his family there."

"But you also know that, when times get tough, people do all kinds of things they declared they would never do."

"I agree, but my answer is still no. I don't think they went to Mexico on the spur of the moment, but what do I know?"

"And you really don't think it's a viable possibility?"

She shrugged. "I don't know anymore. I just don't know what to think at this point."

"So, what about the dog?"

She smiled. "He's a beauty. They named him Thor, but the kids call him Thorny."

"Why Thorny?"

She laughed. "He got caught in one of the big thistle bushes and came in wanting to get loves and cuddles, but he was covered in thorns. It took them quite a while to get all the thorns off him, and he seemed to be quite happy with all the attention he got while it was happening."

"How were the kids with their father?"

She shrugged. "Okay is all I can tell you, but the real answer is, I don't know. Could it have been better? Obviously. Did the kids say anything to me? No," she shared. "And I did try to talk to them before and after they left school for good. I used to go to their house to see how they were doing with their schoolwork and all that, to see if they needed a hand. Most of the time I just got *No, we're fine, thanks* answers. To be honest, over time, the children got a little more distant too, which in my head meant that things were getting uglier at home."

He nodded ever-so-slowly. "That's possible, and that's certainly one potential side effect of something like this," he murmured. "However, that doesn't mean that's how it was though."

"No," she noted, still sounding bitter. "Neither did it reassure me that the kids were doing fine on their own."

He smiled. "I get that. So, who all did you talk to?"

"I spoke to the sheriff. I talked to other neighbors, but apparently Carlos and his family weren't very friendly with the people around here. So a lot of them didn't even know the family and didn't know anything about them. With the family's ties to Mexico, other people are willing to believe the possibility that the family went to Mexico or elsewhere," she suggested. "It's just really hard for me to stop worrying about their abrupt disappearance. I am worried sick about those kids, and I would feel much better knowing that they are safe somewhere."

He nodded. "I wonder if that's a side effect of being a teacher."

She flushed and shook her head. "If it is anything, it's a side effect of being a caring person."

He smiled and nodded. "I won't argue with that. Where would Carlos have gone if he headed to Mexico?"

She looked at him. "You're thinking of going across the border?"

"I don't have a problem with crossing the border," he replied, with a shrug, "if that's what it'll take to find this dog."

"The dog?" she repeated in frustration.

"The family and the War Dog may be together at this point," he acknowledged, with a smile. "That'll be something I have to figure out as well—where they have gone. Then I'll have to see if I can find them."

Hesitating, she added, "Emily didn't say anything to me directly, but somehow I feel they aren't very far from here."

"So why would you assume they did not return to Mexico?"

"Because she told me that she wouldn't ever go back either."

"She may not have had a choice."

"That's my point," Maraya noted immediately, "and it's exactly why I want answers. I'm just afraid that the kids and his wife were taken against their will."

"In which case, we would have to prove that," he pointed out.

"I understand," she replied, "and that's why I'm so frustrated because I don't really know how to do that or have the means to just travel around and look for them. That makes me angry because, right now, it's as if nobody even cares."

"And the kids are really getting to you. I get that."

"Not just them—Emily too," she clarified. "That's particularly difficult."

"In what way?" he asked, studying her intently.

She gave him a small smile and sighed. "I guess because she reminds me of … me."

MARAYA BANKS STUDIED the stranger, not sure why she was even telling him as much as she was, but he was easy to talk to, and something about him compelled her to provide him with all the answers she could. The problem was, she knew next to nothing. "Look," she began. "I never meant to get involved in any of this. I just hoped that somebody could get some answers."

He smiled that same not-quite-neutral smile, one that hid secrets.

She shook her head, as if shaking away a bad thought.

"What?" he asked.

"I didn't even ask you for ID."

"Nope you didn't," he confirmed, a smirk on his face, and handed her his driver's license. "And you invited me, a stranger, over to your place." As she stared at him, he smiled and nodded. "In this case it's okay because I'm safe, but you're right. Taking some basic precautions will serve you well if you ask all the right questions *before* you invite someone over."

She rolled her eyes at him, returning his ID. "Find that dog and you'll find my neighbors," she pointed out.

"And that is definitely a concern, and something that I will look into." He put away his ID. "How was Thorny treated?"

"He was well-loved, well-behaved, and in many ways very protective of the kids."

"Okay, so if Carlos were to do anything to hurt the children, how would Thorny react?"

"I think he would go after the father. He knew the kids before he knew Carlos. I think they applied for the War Dog when he was still overseas, and they got Thorny while Carlos was still deployed. Once he came back, he would have started his own relationship with the dog. However, I just don't see it as being quite the same as the bond the rest of his family had already established with Thorny."

"In which case, if the War Dog did try to intervene," Mateo said, "and Carlos was already having issues, Thorny could be in danger."

"I don't want to think about anything happening to Thorny, but I really don't want anything to happen to those kids either," she declared.

"I hear you, and I'm sorry that this is the situation we're in," he stated, as he stood up and walked around the front porch, as if shaking out his sore legs. "Tell me about the family," he said, pacing lightly.

She looked at him and then shrugged. "You mean, other than what I've just mentioned?"

"Yes," he confirmed. "It's bare minimum as it is. Where does the father work now that he's back? Does Emily work?"

"No, and no," she shared. "They were living off his disability payments."

"Which isn't that much," he pointed out. "And it would be a lot cheaper for them to live in Mexico."

"Maybe, I don't know," she muttered, raising both hands in frustration. "I feel as if I've looked at this from every angle, and nothing makes sense." She shrugged and gave a big sigh. "Maybe they did move to Mexico," she suggested, as she stared off in the distance. "It would have been nice if they had told someone though."

"Sure, but, if Carlos was getting more paranoid and more worried about somebody finding them, worried about being hunted or whatever was going on in his mind at the time, he wouldn't want anybody to know."

"Maybe," she conceded, trying hard to hide her frustration. "That makes sense, but I just don't like it."

He smiled. "And I'm not at all surprised to hear that."

In the distance, they heard a weird bark. She frowned and bolted to her feet, looking in that direction. "Oh my God, that sounds like Thorny, but I don't see him."

"You're kidding," he said, staring at her.

She nodded. "I swear to God it was."

No other barks came. He frowned at her and asked, "Would you have heard that bark before?"

"Sure, lots of times when the kids were out playing. He's got a hell of a bark," she noted, looking around her yard and beyond once more. "I really want to go check out their property."

"Let's go," he agreed immediately. "My truck's over there anyway."

She bolted down the front steps ahead of him and raced over to the neighbor's property again. Either he would follow behind her or he wouldn't. She really didn't know what to think of him, but she was very concerned about Timmy and Donna.

They'd gotten under her skin the whole time she had been teaching them, and losing them to homeschooling had been one thing because she could still see them and could ensure that they were doing okay. Yet, after the children grew quiet and withdrawn, Maraya knew some bigger problems were at home, but the family refused any help. That was a different issue altogether.

As she ran around to the front of the neighbor's property, she stopped, caught her breath, and turned to Mateo, who walked at a more sedate pace, yet at a good clip behind her. "Sorry," she added, when he caught up to her. "I have a tendency to go off in a rush."

"I can see that," he noted, steadying his breath, but he didn't say anything else. His gaze was scanning, taking in the area around them. "Any idea where you think that bark was coming from? Would the dog be over here somewhere?"

"No idea," she admitted, "and it doesn't really make any sense. None of it does, which is part of the reason I'm so concerned about all this."

"Everything will make more sense in the end," he shared, "just not necessarily in a way that you expect with the information available right now."

"At this point, I don't have much in the way of expectations, and that's probably not good either."

He smiled at her. "Let's just see what we can find first."

Together they looped around to the back of the property. He stopped and stared. "They've got quite a few acres here, don't they?"

"I think it's about four," she noted, scanning the unkempt place. "They always wanted land, and they'd had land before, so this just felt like home for them. Emily told me that."

"And that's a good thing," he murmured.

"I just want them happy and free from trouble," she replied. "It's hard when kids are involved. I felt so helpless, knowing they were falling through the cracks like that."

"It's always hard when kids are involved," he agreed. "Particularly in places where Carlos wasn't seeking the support that he needed and could well have been actively refusing it."

"That wouldn't surprise me, especially considering the way they wouldn't even let me help the kids. However, I don't really know, and it's not as if they would confide in me and would open up about what's going on with them."

"Keep in mind that, to them, you're probably seen as the enemy in some ways. You know, with your teacher's mandate to report any worrisome findings regarding the kids."

"I've never been considered the enemy before," she muttered.

"As a teacher? I have no doubt that you are considered the enemy on a semiregular basis," he declared, with a laugh.

She stared at him, surprised to hear the baritone laugh from so deep inside. "That laugh sounds a little rusty," she noted.

He lifted one eyebrow and then nodded. "You could be right," he conceded, as they trampled around the property.

"Is there any reason why we're walking all over out here?" she asked, as they continued to walk. She wasn't leaving him regardless. She just wanted to see what he would do.

"I prefer to see the lay of the land for myself and to figure out what's going on here," he shared.

Maraya nodded, seeing the expression on his face, noting he was perceptive, to say the least.

Mateo continued. "I won't get it figured out in five minutes, but it doesn't hurt to understand the situation better from a geographical point of view. Do they have wheels? A vehicle of some sort?"

"They do have wheels, and it was left behind at first, but now it's gone," she replied. "Last I knew, it wasn't in great running condition, so I doubt it was stolen. More likely it was towed, whether by Carlos or somebody else."

"Was Carlos the kind to go to a mechanic, or could he do the work himself?"

"Yeah, maybe," she added. "I helped Emily get groceries a couple times because she couldn't get the car to start. I saw Carlos tinkering under the hood, so I assumed that he knew the basics at least."

Mateo nodded. "Do you work in town?"

She hesitated, then shrugged. "Yeah, I currently work at one of the dental offices in town."

"I thought you were a teacher." When she shrugged again, he let it go and moved on. "So, the kids, did they go to the dentist?"

"No, never. I even offered free dental care on my nickel at the clinic for them, but Emily wasn't very cooperative in that area. I guess a lot of people don't particularly like dentists."

"A lot of people don't consider them a necessity," he noted, "and others go faithfully. Everybody to their own, I guess."

"And yet I imagine you go."

"Sure, I do," he confirmed, flashing her a smile. "However, I can see why a lot of people don't think much of it. My father would never have gone to the dentist," he shared, with half a smile. "You couldn't have forced him or even bribed him to go."

"And did he have a decent set of teeth at the end?"

"He didn't make it that far," he replied. "Maybe that's why he didn't care. Toward the end, he was more concerned about an easy passing than anything else."

"I'm sorry," she muttered. "It's just another avenue that is easy to get defensive about."

He looked at her and added, "It's probably the red hair."

Her eyes widened, and then she caught his sideways grin and shook her head. "Not too many people would get away with that comment."

At that, he burst out laughing. "And that just proves my point."

She shook her head. "As much as I'm happy that you're having fun here, it's not solving this."

"No," he acknowledged, "but looking around and seeing things for myself will help me picture things in my mind. If you heard Thorny barking just now, and he's still close by, I would guess that the family may be too." He turned to look at the ramshackle house and asked, "How long ago did you notice them missing?"

"*Um,* I think about ten days, a week to ten days I guess."

"Which in many ways isn't a horribly long time," he pointed out.

"No, but how long does it have to be before it's recognized as a problem?" She tried hard to keep the snap out of her tone, but, judging by his expression, she wasn't successful.

He nodded, conceding that point to her, and for whatever reason that made her feel that he was at least listening. Probably not enough to make a difference but it made her feel validated in some ways. "I just really don't want anything to have happened to them."

"If something has happened to them," Mateo noted, "chances are, it's already over with, and it would be a matter of finding the aftermath."

She exhaled before she spoke. "You do realize how horrible that sounds, right?" she pointed out.

"Maybe, but I won't sugar-coat the truth for you just

because it's bad," he shared, facing her. "That is one thing you need to understand."

"No, I get it," she muttered. "You read about this crap all the time in the news. I just was really hoping it wouldn't be *our* news."

"And nothing so far says it'll be your news either," he pointed out. "Let's be clear on that."

She nodded. "I guess, as long as we don't have any answers, the right answer could still be a good one."

"Exactly," he replied. "Let's not get so caught up in the negativity of the moment that the only thing you can think of is something horrible."

"Too late," she mumbled.

He nodded. "I get it, but no sense in letting all those intrusive thoughts go on a rampage in your mind," he said. "You would do better for yourself if you could try to keep some of that under control."

"Trying to keep it under control and succeeding are two different things," she pointed out. They walked the entire property, the fence line, back to the house, and she stayed with him as he went through the house again. She'd obviously interrupted him when she'd arrived earlier.

When he stepped outside again and stared off in the distance, she asked, "So, what's your conclusion?"

"At the moment, nothing more than what you have mentioned. They left in a hurry. Everything is dumped out on the floor, bags unpacked. It's a mess in there. What I don't know is why. I need to check their bank accounts and related things to see if I find any clues there. What about friends?"

She shook her head. "None."

"Carlos's benefits will be automatically deposited into a

bank account, so that's something that could be checked, and, if that's already been done, that would be another reason why nobody is too bothered."

"Yes, but just because bank accounts are recording deposits and withdrawals, that doesn't mean Carlos and his family are the ones using that money."

He eyed her ever-so-slowly. "And do you know of anybody else who would do that?"

She winced. "I don't really like that idea, but, no, I don't know of anyone for sure."

He nodded. "Okay, let's keep that thought, and we'll work on the rest of it first." As he took a few steps away, he pulled out his phone and told her, "I'll just call my boss."

She watched and waited as he made the phone call. He talked in a hushed tone and took about four minutes before rejoining her. "I'll grab a motel in town. I'll be here for a couple days while I figure out what's going on," he explained. "I'll come back here tomorrow to talk to you, if that's all right."

"Sure," she said, "but you can also talk to me now."

"If I had some questions that I needed to ask right now," he explained, "believe me that I would. However, at the moment, we're searching for information, and I'm a little short on questions."

She sighed. "This may sound dumb, but I feel hesitant to let you go, just in case you don't come back again," she admitted, with a tentative smile. "I really want to ensure that somebody is keeping an eye out for them."

"I'm really glad that you are," he stated. "I just wish that every war veteran in the world had somebody confirming he or she was doing okay."

She smiled. "He really was a friendly guy, up until he

came back this last time."

"And you'd seen him before?"

"Yeah," she replied, with a nod. "Back then, they used to come over every once in a while, not too much, and only stayed for half an hour sometimes, but they were friendly, at least as friendly as they could get. There were obviously some barriers, but he was—I don't know. I think he was fine. I was still a teacher, working with his kids at times. However, it was definitely bad at the end of the day."

"Okay," he noted, an odd look on his face as he walked over to his truck. "I'll let you know what I find out."

"Are you sure?"

He frowned at her. "Yes, I'm sure. Why?"

She shrugged. "People say those things all the time, but I worry that, once you leave here, I won't see you again, and I won't get any answers."

He pulled out his phone and asked, "What's your phone number?" She gave it to him immediately. He shook his head and smirked. "You know, I would feel better if you were a little more cautious about giving all your information to a stranger."

She shrugged. "It's a little late for that, considering you already know where I live."

"That's true," he agreed, with a wry smile.

At that moment, another bark came in the distance. He turned in that direction and whispered, "I'll take another walk."

CHAPTER 2

M ARAYA WASN'T SURE what to think about him, but, the minute he heard that bark, he was all business. "You heard it this time too?"

"Yeah, I sure did," he muttered, as he strode off in the direction the barking had come from. "The issue now is whether the dog is in trouble, somebody else is in trouble, the dog is standing guard, or something else entirely is going on," he muttered.

"All of which sounds terrible," she noted.

He smiled at her and gave her a one-arm shrug. "Maybe, but, at least in one sense, it's progress. I definitely heard a bark, and if nobody else around here has dogs—"

"No, we're pretty well the only ones here on this street."

"In that case, we definitely need to find the dog and to see if he's with his family."

She raced to catch up with Mateo and settled into a rougher pace that was just a hair too fast for her. Yet he was stepping out strong, as if he had no health issues. Considering he had shared how he had come back from war himself, she had wondered about that because earlier he hadn't kept up. Still, now he seemed to be doing much better. She asked him, "Are you happy to be back, or did you sign up to go on another tour again?"

"No, I'm back now," he replied, staring at her.

"You mentioned that you understood what Carlos was going through."

"Right," he said, with a nod. "And I do. Nothing quite like being a war vet and finding out that so much of what you thought was your world is now … *different*, for lack of a better word."

She wasn't sure what that meant, but it was obvious that he probably had experiences that most people could not understand or even relate to. "Do you regret going?"

"No, not at all. I wanted to serve my country," he stated, as he kept moving. "I wanted to be part of something bigger."

"And now?" she asked.

"Long and short, I was part of it, and now it's time for a change."

She wanted to ask more questions, but he didn't really seem that open about it. "So, what is it you have in mind?" she asked.

"Lots of things," he said, as he jumped a log and landed awkwardly. "I retrained when I was in the military, got an education, did all kinds of stuff." He gave her a smile. "So many people think you go in and serve for however long, and then you come out with nothing, but that's not true. Some people come out and have way more than they ever had to begin with," he explained.

"And that's you?"

"Yeah, that's me," he confirmed, nodding at her. "You're full of questions. Any particular reason?"

She hesitated and then shrugged. "Maybe because it all just seems odd."

"What does?"

"I don't know," she admitted. "I have the context of

Carlos's family, and he came home in such rough shape. Then there's you, who seems fairly acclimated."

"Everybody is different," he noted. "I spent a lot of time in rehab—not just plain physical rehab but also a lot of psychological retraining too."

And, with that, she realized that he must have had some serious injuries, but he wasn't open to talking about them, and she was being incredibly rude by pushing. "I'm sorry. I don't mean to pry."

He laughed. "Yes, you do," he declared, still chuckling. "You're the kind of gal who likes to know things, but it's just not always that easy for some people to open up."

"You're right," she agreed. "I'm sorry for being pushy."

He just smiled and didn't say anything more.

She continued to keep up as he walked to the very back of the property and then surprised her when he went right over the fence without missing a beat.

"Whose land is this?" he asked her.

"It's government land. Nobody's out here and no buildings either, I understand. As far as I know, it's just wide-open country."

He didn't say much, just kept on moving. She struggled behind him but moved nonetheless. When they got to another fence, he stopped, looked up and down, then clambered over it too.

"You really think the dog is out here?" she asked, as she made it to the other side and jumped down.

"No clue, but let's go find out." When she didn't move, he looked back at her. "You don't have to come with me."

"I'm not giving up now," she snapped. "This is the first day I've heard anything that even resembles Thorny's bark."

He nodded. "And it wasn't just a single bark," he added.

"That was more than a call out. I think it was also a request for help. And that dog is why I'm here. So believe me that I'll be looking for him."

She felt an irrational level of disappointment that he would care more about the dog than the people. And it was hard for her to not lash out, but she managed to keep her tone somewhat modulated when she spoke up, "And that's it? When you find the dog, you leave?"

He shook his head. "Not necessarily, it depends on what I find," he replied. "Why don't we just park all these *what ifs* and see what we find first?" And, with that, he strode ahead of her into the pasture across from her house.

She had barely even remembered that a pasture was here, and it had been a long time since she'd been anywhere near this area.

He asked her, "When was the last time you were over here?"

"I'm not sure I ever have been here. Not on the land itself, just seeing it maybe. I was just thinking about that," she murmured, as she moved forward. "It's not necessarily an area that I would go into. I have lots of land myself, so I don't need to trample on somebody else's."

"Right," he noted. "So you aren't somebody who always needs to have more and more."

"Nope," she murmured, "definitely not that. But it would be nice to know that nothing is out here, at least nothing wrong."

THAT BARK FROM the dog was something instinctive. It bothered Mateo to hear it because it was not a normal bark, more like calling for help, responding to whatever. Maraya refused to go home, and he understood that. However, her questions were getting to him. Mostly because he had tried to stomp down all her fears and to not worry about this. Even in therapy, everybody kept asking questions he didn't want to deal with. Most of the time, questions were fine, but, every once in a while, they got a little too close for comfort, and then he wasn't happy with it.

On the other hand, Maraya was doing pretty well at keeping up with him, and her concern was evident. So, if she had that kind of a relationship with Carlos and his family, then she and Mateo could potentially be walking into something difficult for her to deal with. Even still, he could only hope that they would find the dog he heard and that it was in fact Thorny and not some stray.

He wasn't sure what he was supposed to do after that. It would be hard to walk away, but, if the police hadn't found anything to support the missing family theory, Mateo wasn't sure what he could do. And yet the part of him that had spent the last many years helping other people was also telling him that he couldn't just walk away from this. Easy to say but harder to do.

As he strode across the land, he stopped several times to look back and wait for her.

She glared at him. "I'm fine."

"Good."

"How far away do you think Thorny is?" she asked.

"We don't know if that's Thorny barking, and I have no idea how far away the dog is. I was hoping we would hear it bark another time while we were out here."

"Good God," she muttered. "So, we'll be out here until we hear it again?"

"Maybe," he replied, with a shrug. "We have a limited amount of daylight to find the dog. And then it'll get much worse."

"*Great*," she muttered.

As she stepped up beside him, he smiled. "You're holding up really well."

"Doesn't feel like it," she muttered. "I had a car accident a few years ago, so I'm not in quite the shape that I wish I was."

"Accidents can really take it out of you," he murmured. "Yet you're back up on your feet, and you're moving, so that's all good."

"It is, but it wasn't an easy battle."

"Nothing like that ever is," he stated, smiling, as she eyed him skeptically. "And, yes, I do know that firsthand."

She nodded. "Some of your movement is a little stiff."

"Spine surgery, couple ribs missing, spleen missing, chunk of my liver gone," he shared cheerfully. "It's a good thing livers grow back. Regardless I'm not quite the same man I used to be."

"No, but I imagine in many ways you're a lot better."

He smiled at her and gave a small nod. "And that … is very true."

Just then, as they were about to come up to another fence, they heard the bark again, off ever-so-slightly to the side. Mateo immediately turned in that direction, scanning the field in front of him.

"It's lonely out here," she muttered, searching. "It's completely empty, … as if absolutely nothing is here."

"And probably not very much is out here," he replied, "but obviously something is." He turned to her, and her expression was not positive. "You look worried."

She shook her head. "It's not that I'm worried as much as this is just a very odd circumstance."

"It is, no doubt about that," he confirmed.

"And now the bigger problem is, what will we do about it?"

"Let's find the dog first, and we'll go from there." And, with that, he strode ahead, making sure that she was behind him, but he wasn't exactly waiting for her.

She stayed abreast, and, by the time he got over to where he thought he heard the dog, he stopped and waited. There was nothing, absolutely nothing. "It's almost like a trick," she whispered beside him, "as if somebody else was here, using the dog to bring us in—"

He shook his head, staring at her for a long moment. "I won't say that's not possible because it certainly is," he admitted, "but it's not something I want to consider right now."

"Sorry," she added, "and I didn't really mean it as being something wrong right now either. It's just—I don't know." She shrugged. "As I said, I have a very weird feeling out here right now."

"Did the family ever have many visitors?"

"I didn't really keep track, and, when I did see visitors, I think it was mostly deliveries and stuff, but what do I know?"

"Friends?"

"No, I don't think so. I remember a fight, and Carlos was chasing somebody off his property a while back. However, for all I know, Carlos got so weird that he was chasing off good people, just wanting to help. Now that he's not the same person, he may very well have decided he didn't like anyone being around."

"It's possible."

No further bark came from the dog, so Mateo moved forward cautiously, wondering exactly what he had heard and whether the dog was calling out or if it was being evasive because it also wasn't sure about who or what was coming closer.

"Why won't it bark now?" she whispered.

"Because he's not sure he can trust us." With that, Mateo sent out a long whistle, and then he waited.

She frowned at him for a moment and asked, "Was that some secret code?"

He smiled. "Depends on whether the dog was trained to that whistle or not." Within a minute came a sudden series of sharp barks. He nodded. "That means, either he's willing to take a chance or he does recognize that whistle." And Mateo strode carefully forward.

"Do we need to be worried about something else?" she asked.

"I don't have an answer for you," he admitted, glancing at her, and then moved forward again. "If they're missing, and we now have a dog barking in the distance, and a dog was in their life that also went missing with them, I would think that this is probably our best bet, but I do understand your concern."

"Oh God, that was foolish. I mean, right now, I feel really stupid for even bringing it up."

"Don't ever do that," he said, turning to her. "We never really know what's going on, but, if there's a chance to find answers about the dog and potentially the family, and they are just a heartbeat away, that is worth continuing for."

"I agree, which is why I'm here with you, but it's all a little surreal."

"It's a lot surreal," he stated, "and it's a lot to take in, but we have to keep moving."

CHAPTER 3

MARAYA SLAMMED INTO Mateo as he stopped suddenly in front of her. "What is it?" she asked.

But he grabbed her, asking for silence.

She peered over his shoulder and froze because, sure enough, Thorny appeared to be up ahead, and he was growling and barking at something they couldn't see, something just out of their sight.

He pushed her back behind him. "Stay here."

She wanted to argue, but she figured Mateo could see a little bit more than she could. He suddenly disappeared up ahead of her into the shrubbery. Hearing an odd bark again, she huddled behind a tree and tried to peer around it, looking for some idea of what was upsetting Thorny. He was growling and gave a loud series of barks and howls that kind of terrorized her.

She froze, wondering just what the hell was going on and what she was supposed to do about it. Just then, right when she was about to head closer to see if she could do something to help, silence fell. She stayed where she was until Mateo called out, "Maraya, it's okay. Come on out here."

She froze at that but took a cautious step forward, then another and another. As she got closer, she saw Thorny lying on the ground, his tail wagging, and right beside him was a small body. She raced forward. "Oh my God, this is Timmy."

Mateo looked up at her and nodded. "And he's in bad shape. … That's why the dog was calling out but was still hesitant, not knowing who was friend and who was foe."

She looked over at Thorny and called out to him by name. Immediately he whined and crept closer. She gave him a hug and a cuddle. She looked over as Mateo carefully checked the boy over. "Do you know what you're doing?" she asked, her tone sharp but low.

"As much as I don't want to have this knowledge, I do have a lot of field medic experience."

She noted Timmy shivering uncontrollably and winced at that. "Should I call 9-1-1? They won't come to us here. We'll have to get him back to the road."

"You do that. This little boy is unconscious, looks dehydrated, and I don't see or feel any injuries, like broken bones. I'm not sure why he's here, but if he—" He turned to look, as if searching for something.

"Something wrong?" she asked.

"I hope not. It's weird that he's alone—"

She paled at that. "I just don't get that part," she whispered, a stutter in her tone. With her phone now ringing madly in her hand, she frowned.

"You need to turn down the volume. It doesn't look like he's been attacked or anything."

"I just don't understand why he's here. This makes no sense at all. It's so random."

"It is random," he agreed, "but *random* doesn't necessarily tell us anything."

She groaned. "I really, really want some answers."

He smiled and nodded. "Of course you do. Who was on

the phone?"

"A friend I don't really want to talk to right now. I'll call 9-1-1 for help."

Her phone call was answered by the dispatcher in the sheriff's office. Maraya quickly explained what they had found. With a promise of help on the way, she ended the call and turned to look back at him. "They're sending an ambulance."

"Good," he replied, but his gaze was in the distance.

"What's going on now?" she whispered, as she stepped up closer but stayed within a foot or two of Timmy's prone body.

"I don't know," he admitted, "but my best guess is that he hasn't been here all that long."

"Oh God," she whispered, as the reality sunk in. "You think somebody saw us out here and left the boy here for us to find? How is that even possible?"

He raised his eyebrows and shook his head. "I'm not sure."

"Right." She scrubbed her face and then bent down beside Timmy. "Do you think it's safe to move him? We could carry him back to my place. That's where the ambulance will come."

"We're quite a way out here." He hesitated, looked back, and nodded. "I can go get help."

"I'm not sure I want to leave him alone or to be alone out here either." She glared at him, and Mateo nodded. "I know, Timmy first."

He looked down at the little boy and announced, "I'll carry him. You lead the way."

She hesitated, but he shot her a look, and she quickly got to her feet as he bent down, scooped up the little boy's limp body, and said, "Let's go."

And, with that, she led the way back to her place, Thorny following closely behind them. They had reached the back of her property when she heard the sirens. Only a few minutes more and little Timmy was in safe hands, and the police were all over her and Mateo. When she recognized a deputy she knew because she had taught his kids, he just stared at her. Confused expressions were all around. "I told you all something was wrong, Rodney."

He nodded. "You did tell us, but you couldn't give us any details," he clarified. "So obviously things are a whole lot worse than we thought they were." She just shook her head, so angry that it was hard for her to talk. Rodney turned and looked over at Mateo. "What brought you here?" he asked, suspicion in his tone.

She turned to Rodney and frowned at him in shock. "He's from the War Department, here to check on the War Dog," she snapped. "At least somebody gives a shit."

He glared at her. "That's enough, all right? We have only so many man-hours, and we found absolutely nothing. It's not as if this little boy has been lying out there this whole time."

"No," she snapped, "it's not. I highly doubt that he's been there very long at all."

"Maybe," Rodney replied, "and that's something we can get into now." He turned and looked back at Mateo. "I asked what you were doing here."

Mateo stared at him for a long moment and then nodded. "I came looking for Thorny," he replied.

Rodney snorted. "You came looking for a dog?"

Mateo raised his eyebrows and clarified, "I came looking for a War Dog that served his country and that deserves better than to be tossed into the brink, just as some rescue dog to be adopted."

Rodney flushed angrily. "Not all of us could take off and fight in the war."

"And not all of us who did deserve to be criticized."

"I didn't say anything about you," Rodney retorted. "You're just taking offense where there isn't any."

"Oh, come on, Rodney," Maraya snapped, staring at him. "You came here with a chip on your shoulder already. What the hell is going on?"

"Nothing," he declared, turning back to Mateo. "We'll need to get your statement down at the station."

"You can get my statement now," he offered, crossing his arms and leaning against her vehicle.

Rodney wasn't happy with that answer. He stared at him and struggled to come up with something else to say, but something was very intimidating about Mateo, the way he stood, the way he acted.

It was an interesting dynamic that she wasn't used to seeing, but no doubt Rodney was affected by it. She looked over at Mateo and suggested, "Maybe we should both go in tomorrow."

"We could," Mateo noted. "I do want to see the case files for the search they did for the family."

"You don't get to see the case files," Rodney snapped. "You don't have any jurisdiction here. You're not a cop. You're nobody."

"Hey, hey, hey, easy, Rodney," Xavier, the second deputy finally spoke up, as he came over to see what was going on. "The little boy looks as if he'll be okay," he shared, smiling at Maraya. "You guys found him just in time."

"And how very convenient that you found him at all,"

Rodney snapped.

She immediately stiffened and glared at him. "What do you mean by that?" she asked him. "And you better watch what you say."

At that, Xavier again shushed his partner and explained, "Look. Rodney's just a little overwrought. We all are. I apologize for Rodney. I am Xavier," he announced, looking at Mateo.

"Mateo Montgomery."

Xavier nodded. "So, we did come out and searched the house, but absolutely nothing revealed what was going on and certainly not that a little boy was out in the field—though he obviously hasn't been here all that long. Otherwise, he would be in much worse shape."

Rodney frowned at Mateo.

Instinctively she knew what he would say. "Don't bother," she snapped, repeating, "Mateo's willing to give you a statement right now but don't keep pushing."

"We're not pushing," Rodney declared. "When a stranger shows up, and all of a sudden a kid appears in the middle of the field behind the home of a family who's been missing for a week and a half, it's suspicious."

She looked at him in shock. "Is that what you've come up with? I've been asking you to come out here and to do a deeper investigation since this thing started, and nobody's given a crap," she snapped, staring at the two men who she'd known for years. "Mateo just arrived in town a few hours ago. And this is all you have to say?"

"No, it's not all we have to say," Rodney spat, glaring at her. "I told you. Don't go off with that crazy attitude again."

"Easy, easy," Xavier told his partner. "This kind of talk will have a bad ending, and we don't need that. Everybody needs to calm down."

"Yeah, just calm down, Deputy," Mateo stated, his arms still crossed. "Interesting system you have here. Seems to me you prefer to beat down and barrage witnesses who don't have anything to do with the actual matter at hand. Can't say I was expecting a hero's welcome for finding the lost boy," he added, with a touch of self-mockery, "but the fact that you're looking at us as being involved in the family going missing is very interesting."

"What do you mean, *interesting*?" Rodney snapped, glaring at him. "We've got a little boy who just showed up out of nowhere in rough shape."

"And so I must have had something to do with it because I'm new in town, is that it?" Mateo asked, one eyebrow raised.

Rodney flushed. "We sure as hell didn't have any inkling that he was out here before now, and suddenly you show up and find him out of the blue. So yeah, that's fairly strange." Rodney stated.

"Maybe if you had been one of those out here looking …" Mateo began.

Xavier stared at Rodney, raising a hand. "That won't get us anywhere, Rodney," he repeated. He looked over at Maraya. "Obviously things are a little heated right now, so it's probably best we take this to the station."

She shook her head. "I feel as if I don't even know you guys right now," she admitted, feeling half numb. "This is not at all the response I expected."

"Of course not," Rodney snapped, staring at her. "Looks as if you've sided with the devil."

"I haven't sided with anybody," she stated, turning to stare at him in shock. "You know perfectly well how worried

I've been about this family and how completely uncaring you've been yourselves."

"That's not true," he protested. "We have a lot of cases and a lot of issues in town that need solving, not just the ones you are worried about," he declared, giving her a hard look.

She snorted. "Yet, when we do find the little boy, instead of setting up a search for the rest of the family now, you only want our statements and can't be bothered to do anything else."

Rodney muttered, "Oh, you *found* the little boy all right."

"Good—that's great. We'll mark that down as done and move on," she replied, her tone mocking. "Why the hell is there not a full-on search going on right now for the rest of the family?"

Rodney blushed, as Xavier looked at her in shock. "Do you really believe the rest of the family's out there?"

"How the hell would I know? How the hell would you know if you don't go looking for them?" she exploded. "We heard Thorny bark. That's the War Dog. We went out there looking for the dog, and we found him with the little boy, and that's all I know. The fact that you're not doing more even right after we found Timmy is what really concerns me right now."

"Don't worry about it. This is our job, we'll handle it."

"You'll handle it as well as you handled their disappearance in the first place, right?" she asked in disgust. At that, Rodney stiffened. "Yeah, I know what you'll say, what you always say," she stated. "You want me to keep my mouth shut and just let you do your thing."

"Yeah, and it's for the best if you do that," Rodney

snapped. "We do know what we're doing."

"You sure as hell can't prove it by me," she stated, glaring at him.

"And you're getting a little bit too mouthy for your own good," Rodney snapped right back. "You might want to watch that."

She stared at him for a long moment. "And what the hell does that mean?"

"Nothing," he said, sharing a snide remark under his breath with his buddy. "Come on. We've got to go."

"Go where?" Mateo asked. "Maraya's right. Why are you not organizing a search right now for the rest of the family?"

"It's none of your business what we do here," Rodney spat, frowning at him. "In case you haven't figured it out, we don't like strangers, particularly strangers who all of a sudden show up and cause trouble."

"Cause trouble?" Mateo repeated, an eyebrow raised. "That's a very interesting analogy. I mean, considering we just found a little boy who's been lost for a week and a half?"

Rodney turned to glare at Maraya.

She nodded. "That's it exactly," she told Mateo, "not that these guys care." And, with that, she turned and stormed off to her porch.

"We still need you to come in and give your statement."

"Yeah, yeah, yeah." She gave them a backhand wave. She raised her voice as she continued to walk away from them. "Interesting how that's all on your time schedule but still *not right now*. Of course, if you were out doing a real search, then I would understand, but you're not. So I really don't see why I have to go down to the station rather than give you my statement here and now."

He stared at her for a long moment. "I could always arrest you and take you in."

She slowly turned and looked at him. "You and who else?" Her tone was soft, dangerously soft.

Immediately Mateo stepped forward. Stepping between them, he interjected, "Not sure exactly what kind of a problem we've got here that this is the reception she's dealing with, but I'll be sure to pass it on to my superiors."

At that, Xavier looked at him and asked, "Who are you?"

"I already told you who I am and why I'm here. I came here on behalf of the War Department to look for Thorny," he repeated, "and I'm finding a very interesting and troubling situation here."

Xavier suddenly looked very uncomfortable. "Come on, buddy." He motioned at Rodney, then turned to Maraya. "Look. Everybody's pretty hot-headed right now," he added. "If you could come down to the station tomorrow, we'll take your statement and record it, like everything else. Other than that, no need for people to get agitated."

She stared at him and shook her head. "*Right*, though I would think you would want to notify little Timmy's family that he's been found. Oh, wait. You don't know where they are. So at least maybe notify every other parent in town that there's no need to *get agitated* when a little boy shows up unconscious out of the blue in the backwoods, all alone with a dog who's also been missing with the rest of the family for ten days. Nothing here to get worried or agitated about. I mean, absolutely no reason, right?"

He flushed. "Now look—"

She waved him off and shared, "I'll show up tomorrow morning when things are a little calmer, but you better ensure that Rodney is calmer too and that the sheriff is there as well."

"Of course he will be." Rodney glared at her. "Why wouldn't he be?"

She laughed. "You and I both know why he wouldn't be. So, let's just ensure everything is fine and dandy before this blows up any further."

"It ain't blowing anywhere," Rodney argued. "You've got nothing to stand on." And, with that, Rodney strode over to his vehicle, looked back at them, and added, "Make sure you're in town tomorrow."

"Oh, I will be," Mateo confirmed, with a smile. "Absolutely."

Frowning, the two deputies looked at each other, shrugged, got into their vehicle, and took off.

She turned to Mateo and asked, "What the hell is going on here?"

"You tell me," he said. "That was a very strange reception for finding a little boy who's been missing all this time."

"I know," she agreed, "and it doesn't make any sense."

"And apparently you have some history with the local law enforcement."

"Yeah, well, that's because the sheriff is my ex-husband," she muttered, "and believe me, that won't make anything better."

"So why do you want him there when you go in tomorrow?"

"Because he absolutely hates when I get into trouble, as he feels his reputation *suffers* somehow."

"His reputation will suffer because his ex-wife found a little lost boy?" Mateo asked, shaking his head. "I really don't get it. I'm not sure what's going on, but I don't really like any of it."

"Yeah, you and me both," she muttered. She stared off

in the distance. "I want to go back out there and look for the family."

"Glad you mentioned that," he replied, "because I want to do that too." He looked down at the dog, smiled, and added, "And so does he."

She smiled, reached over to pat Thorny. "Thank you so much for looking after Timmy," she whispered to him. He barked and wagged his tail in a reckless, happy manner.

"At least somebody is happy to have him back," she muttered, as she stared off in the distance. "I think it must be my relationship with my ex that's causing the attitude."

"I don't understand. That was all very strange."

"I know. It was strange even for me," she muttered, "so I don't know what's going on." She looked at him and asked, "Will the War Department back you up?"

"Oh yeah," he said, with a smile, "and so will my bosses, believe me. They'll be very upset to hear about the cavalier attitude that this little boy's rescue has received and how nobody is interested in coming out and searching for clues about the other members of Timmy's family."

"I think that's the part that really drives me nuts. Why doesn't anybody out here care?" she cried out softly. Thorny, hearing the pain in her voice, whined and came closer to her. She bent down and gave him a big hug. "It's not your fault, big guy. You kept Timmy alive and let us know that he was there," she whispered.

"Do you know anybody on the local search and rescue team?"

She hesitated and then shrugged. "It's usually people from the sheriff's department. My ex is big on that too."

He nodded. "Okay, so would you *not* want to contact any of them and let them know?"

She looked at him. "I could, but I don't have any authority. Plus, I don't know that anybody will care though."

"You would like to think that they do," Mateo noted, shaking his head. "I'll contact my boss and have a talk with him about what just went down. Something very strange is going on here, and I don't particularly like the way it's panning out."

"You and me both," she muttered, staring at him. "It's not exactly what I would have thought was normal behavior."

"It isn't," Mateo declared, "but short of their having had something to do with the family's disappearance in the first place—"

"I don't think so," she interrupted, "but I do think there's a lack of empathy from anybody in town. And, to be honest, Carlos has gotten kind of wild in town and has made a mess with people."

"Meaning, he was violent?"

She nodded. "I know Emily tried really hard to keep him calm and quiet, but once in a while he would go into town, he'd get some liquor, and that would be it." He just nodded at that. "You're not surprised?"

"Booze is an easy way to forget for a time, isn't it?" he asked, looking at her with a wry smile. "It's not the best way, but it's often a choice people make."

"I suppose," she muttered. "I just know that he gets pretty scary when he gets angry. It's ugly."

"Most people do," Mateo stated. "Most people do."

She stared at him and added. "The deputies had a very strange reaction to you, I thought."

He smiled and nodded. "Yeah, they did," he confirmed, as he pushed away from her vehicle. "I'm really wondering about that too."

"Is there any reason why they would treat you that way?" she asked, looking at him.

"I don't know," he admitted, "but I'm really looking forward to finding out."

MATEO SPOKE WITH Badger and Kat at length, both of them mystified at the attitude. "Not sure what's going on, and I'm pretty sure nobody will let me see any files," Mateo added, "and that'll just piss me off but—"

At that, Badger laughed. "God, we're all the same. … We all want in, even though we're not entitled to be in."

"Of course," Mateo murmured. "I mean, when shit is going on that we don't understand, we just automatically want the information so we can figure it out. I just don't understand, and none of it makes any sense. Anyway, we're heading back out to search again now, although it'll be dark before long."

"And nobody from search and rescue is out there to back you up?"

"No, it's almost as if they knew nobody else would be there," Mateo offered. "That's the part I find very suspicious."

"Oh, it is very suspicious," Kat confirmed.

Mateo heard paperwork rustling on the other end. "What are you looking for in your magic little book there? I hope you are trying to muster someone to back me up here."

The rustling stopped, and then she asked, "How did you know?"

"Because that's just what you would do."

"I sent you out there, so believe me that I won't take it kindly if any issues are there. I'm really having trouble with the attitude toward the family," she hesitated.

"Me too. Are you thinking it's because of their Mexican background?"

"I'm just saying it's a possibility."

Mateo sighed. "It's not the first time I've faced racism."

"It still shouldn't be happening, especially not in the situation we are in."

"Nope, it shouldn't. I haven't faced it in a long time because, in the military, in my case in particular, it wasn't an issue. Maybe it was for others. I don't know." He gave a groan and admitted, "Can't say the leg and the back are appreciating this."

"That's because you're supposed to have another surgery and maybe fix it," she pointed out. "And, if that doesn't work, you're coming to me."

"And I'm trying hard *not* to come to you," he stated, with a laugh.

"I know, and I understand. I get it. You're not quite ready to come my way."

"Nope, I'm sure not," he shared. "I've been working with Badger's group for quite a while now though, and it's nice to remember good things about people instead of coming here, where you get reminded about the shitty things."

"And that just pisses me off," Kat stated. "So, you watch your back now. I don't know what's going on there, but best to be on your guard."

"I have no idea either," he agreed, "but the fact is, a little boy is in the hospital and is hopefully getting care now, and that's a comfort."

"And that's something I'll check up on too," she murmured. "If nothing else, we might have a doctor there."

"That would be a help. Any inside track you could give us would be good."

"Us?" she asked, her tone a little sharp. "Who else is there?"

"Yeah, you told me to talk with Maraya. She lives near the missing family and has been checking up on them this whole time. Thorny recognized her as well."

"Good," Kat replied, a note of humor in her tone. "You just never know who you'll meet when you come to these places."

"*Ha.* Don't you go matchmaking."

"Never," she replied instantly.

Badger snorted at that. "Too late, buddy," he told Mateo. "You might as well just give in now."

"I don't know Maraya very well," Mateo pointed out, "so that ain't happening."

"Doesn't matter. As far as Kat's concerned, every stranger out there is just a friend you haven't met yet." And, with that, Badger ended the call.

Mateo stared down at the phone and shook his head.

"Problems?" Maraya asked, as she walked toward him, a heavier jacket around her shoulders, and he realized that a chill had set in.

"No," he said, with a smile. "Just talked to the bosses. They'll do what they can. They're good people."

"That's good to hear," she muttered. "I never really know who's good and who's not anymore."

"And yet you were married to the sheriff," he noted, looking at her.

"I was, and that wasn't exactly a smart move on my part."

"And why is that?"

She gave him a glance and sighed. "Now you're asking personal questions."

"It seems only fair, since that's what you've been doing too."

She winced and shook her head. "Yeah, okay, point taken."

He smiled. "Ready to go?"

"I am. It'll get dark soon."

"It will, but I figure we can go back out to the same area and see what else is there, see where Thorny leads us. Now that we have the little boy safe and sound, it will be interesting to see if Thorny picks up on anything else."

She nodded as they headed out. "I married Riley—that's the sheriff—because I was pregnant with his brother's child," she shared, "and he promised to look after me and his nephew, but it didn't work out that way." He frowned at her. She shrugged and continued. "I was young and stupid, and I wanted to believe that somebody would be there to help."

"And he wasn't?"

"No, he just got insanely jealous and angry because it was his brother's child and not his."

"And the father?"

She frowned, didn't answer for a long moment, then shook her head. "He was in a car accident, soon after we graduated high school," she explained. "I was already heavily pregnant at the time. The families on both sides were pretty excited. I just didn't think I could handle being a single parent. I was devastated and looking for a place to land," she said, waving her hand. "Riley and I got married immediately, and, well, … let's just say it was a stupid idea."

"And the baby?" he asked. Her steps faltered, and he knew the answer would not be good news. "I'm sorry."

"Me too," she muttered. "I was really hoping I could have the child to remember his father by, but God had other plans. I miscarried him, and, if I had just waited, I wouldn't have ended up married to Riley. And, of course, once I was married, and all the dust had settled, I didn't want to stay married, and things just became even uglier. Particularly after a second miscarriage."

"I'm sorry."

"No, it's my fault," she admitted. "I was stupid and young, and I was grieving. When you're doing all those things at once, you are not equipped to make big decisions, or at least you shouldn't make them." She shook her head. "I did, and I shouldn't have, and I paid the price."

"Was he ever physically abusive?"

"He was getting that way, slapping me around. He did scare the crap out of me one day, and I told him that I was done and that if he ever spoke to me that way or came at me with his fist again like he did, I would have him charged. Riley wasn't the sheriff at the time. He was eight years older than I was, old enough to know better. He says he always wanted what his brother had, and that's why he married me. Not exactly a basis for a healthy long-term marriage, and, of course, it didn't work out because I was still in love with Joseph, his dead brother. Riley was never in love with me," she noted, with a shrug. "And life goes on."

"I'm sorry. That sounds like a real mess."

She laughed. "That's a hell of a good way to put it. I've lived here all my life, and I never wanted to leave. A couple times I've thought about it, but, once you own a place, it's hard."

"And sometimes it's the best answer," he pointed out. "It's a clean break, and you get to move on."

"And I've thought about it a couple times since," she shared, "but I never really made the move. I didn't have any reason to."

"You still want to stay?"

She shrugged. "Let's just say I haven't had a pressing reason to leave, but, if a compelling reason arose, I would leave." He just nodded. She looked over at him and asked, "You?"

"I'd been helping to build houses for vets when I was asked to pick up this War Dog job," he replied, with a smile. "I've been at odds after the surgeries and rehab. It's one of those things. Just like what you said, … you shouldn't make big decisions until you're ready. And then, when you make decisions, things happen very quickly."

"I guess I'm gun-shy and stuck in the *not making any decisions* stage," she muttered. "Didn't have a reason to, I guess."

"Do you like your job?"

"Yes, but it's also often very frustrating. The townsfolk are very conservative. The people questioned my motives and choices all the time," she shared. "I've often thought about moving to a bigger place where I would have better opportunities. I would love to teach special ed, but we don't have enough budget here for me to focus on that. And kids here really need it, but it's hard because there's no time or money for it."

"I think that's probably the same everywhere."

"Yes, but there are definitely places where there is more money," she noted. "So, it's one of those *maybe someday* kind of things."

"Ah." Mateo nodded. "I have a few of those *maybe some-day things* too."

They kept walking, and their pace was clipped and fast because of the cold and the approaching nightfall. She murmured, "Do you really think anybody else is out here? The conditions aren't very favorable for it."

"I don't know," he said. "I did bring a flashlight, but I'm hoping Thorny will be our best lead."

She glanced down at Thorny and smiled. "He seems to be totally happy."

"He handed off his young charge, and, in his world, people direct him. So it makes sense that he's comfortable right now." Mateo gave him a smile. "But we do need to know where the rest of his family is, and I need to figure out what's happening with Thorny from here on out," he added.

"He can stay with me temporarily," she offered. "I don't know that I'm, you know, the right person for a War Dog by any means. I'm really surprised that this family got him."

"It probably had to do with Carlos's status as a veteran. Maybe it was a dog he knew while he served. There are all kinds of potential reasons for it," he noted, with a smile. "I don't even know what the criteria is, but, as long as the animals are taken care of, it's okay with me."

She smiled at that. "It sounds to me as if you're more happy-go-lucky than anything right now."

"I would say not so much happy-go-lucky but still not committed to a new direction in life."

"That could be tough too," she said, looking at him. "Most of us have priorities, commitments, and other things that keep us grounded."

"Absolutely," he agreed.

"Where do you work again?"

"I was helping build homes for severely injured soldiers and their families," he explained. "That's what I was doing. I was just talking to my boss about potentially taking on a supervisory role and growing the operation a little bit bigger because there's such a need for the disabled veterans to have accessible homes."

"I hadn't even considered that," she admitted. "I guess they come back and can't necessarily work, can they?"

"Some come back and can. Some come back and can't." He shrugged. "Every case is completely different, and, because it's so individual, there are just no real easy answers for a blanket budget."

"Right," she muttered. "I really like the idea that you are doing that work." She gave him a smile. "I always wanted to help more, but you never really know what that entails or in what way to start. Besides working at the dental office, I tutor in the evenings, and I've helped lots of other kids get their grades up so that they can go on to university and college, much to the disgust of some of the families."

"Meaning?"

"As I mentioned, it's a fairly conservative area. It's not necessarily a career-driven town, and people around here don't always appreciate the intrusions of higher education. I did have one mom ask what the point would be of her daughter getting an education if she would just get married and have babies. She was pissed at the whole idea of *college preparation.*"

He stared at her and asked, "Really?"

"Yeah, really," she confirmed, with a wince. "I can understand that mind-set from thirty or forty years ago, but today? It's a hard attitude to accept. Not only a hard attitude," she said, "but it's very backward, and this is what the kids are raised with sometimes around here, and it's hard for them."

"Of course it is. They're also bucking everything they've been raised with, and that makes it even worse."

"Absolutely." As they walked forward, she asked, "Is there any way to get Thorny to search or to at least look around?"

"I'm hoping when we get into the area, he'll be more active in this hunt that we've got going on," he shared, as he looked down at the dog. Just then Thorny froze, his ears lifted, and he woofed softly, but it was half-bark and half-growl. "Kind of like that," he whispered. "I'm not too sure what's going on, but something is up, and it's not something he's particularly fond of."

"And that could be anything," she whispered back, "from a bear to coyotes or anything in-between."

"Exactly," he agreed, looking at her. "It's the in-between part that we have to worry about."

And, with that, he stepped forward and warned in a low voice, "Stay close behind me."

CHAPTER 4

T HE WIND HAD picked up to the point that Maraya had her jacket pulled up tight around her neck, as she and Mateo crept forward into the growing darkness. Now she wished that she was home, safe and sound and out of whatever this was, and yet Mateo didn't seem bothered in the least. He moved smoothly, a little stiffly at times, but, if he'd had back surgery, no wonder. She crept forward, peering through the woods along with him. "I don't see anything," she whispered.

He shook his head. "Neither do I, but it doesn't mean a whole lot because this guy does." He pointed at the War Dog.

She looked down to see Thorny still staring straight ahead, emitting a low growl that was enough to raise the hairs on the back of her head. "I hate it when he does that," she muttered.

Mateo smiled and nodded. "And yet it's a warning system, one that we need to heed. So, it doesn't matter whether we like it or not. … This is very much something we need to be aware of." He stepped forward a little bit more, then took another step and another. All of a sudden, Thorny froze again, then barked ferociously and tore off into the woods.

She didn't even have time to register that he was gone before Mateo yelled back at Maraya, "Stay here." And he tore off after the dog.

"Stay here," she muttered to herself, as she stared around in the growing darkness. "Are you serious? It's freaking scary out here, and no way I want to be out here alone." And yet she wasn't sure where to go or how to handle it. Suddenly Mateo was right there beside her again.

"It's okay," he whispered.

"What do you mean, it's okay?" she asked, staring up at him. "What the hell was that?"

"I don't know. Thorny took off in the brush and was moving too fast for me to catch up. I didn't want to leave you all alone, so I came back."

"Thank you. It all caught me by surprise, so I appreciate the sentiment," she murmured, as she stared at him. "But what the hell is going on?"

"I don't know, but it's something bizarre. Yet, at the moment, I can't tell you what."

SOON THORNY RETURNED to them, and Mateo quickly turned her around and hustled her as fast as he could back to the house.

"You're really rushing me," she complained.

"I am in a way," he admitted. "It's cold, it's dark, and whatever was out there is gone. I'll go back tomorrow and see if I can find out who and or what it was."

"And yet you don't want to do it now? Why?"

"We're not prepared for these conditions, like the temperature," he noted. "It came up fast, and I don't want you becoming another casualty here." She winced at that. He smiled, then nodded. "My focus is to ensure everything with the dog is okay, but I won't sacrifice anybody else just because we need to figure out some things. Right now we need to take a step back."

"*Ha.* It's more than just a need to figure out things. Definitely something very strange is going on here. The fact that Timmy is alive says a lot."

"We need to check on him too," he pointed out.

"He's been on my mind," she admitted ruefully. "I was thinking, as soon as we got back, maybe I should make a trip to the hospital. Not to mention we also have to go in and give a statement at some point." She groaned at that.

He smiled and nodded. "It won't be too bad."

"Are you kidding me?" she snapped. "Anything to do with my ex is painful. Riley doesn't make it easy."

"On your side or his?"

"Meaning what exactly?" she asked, frowning at him in confusion.

"Are you still dealing with emotions on your side, or is he dealing with emotions on his?"

"He's dealing with anger on his side. I'm not sure whether or not anything else is going on," she grumbled. "On my side, I'm free and clear and intend to stay that way. It has been a while, but Riley just hasn't been good at letting sleeping dogs lie."

Mateo didn't say anything to that.

She shrugged. "I don't know whether he'll make a scene tomorrow or not, but just the thought of having to go in on his turf is enough to make me nervous."

"I'll be there with you," he reminded her, "so I don't imagine he'll make too much of a stink."

"You don't know him," she pointed out, "and it won't matter to him if you are there or not." He stared at her, and she shook her head. "As I told you, he's not a happy camper in general, and he's definitely not happy with me."

"So either he still has strong emotions or he hasn't dealt with his issues."

"Maybe, but I'm unwilling for his drama to be my issue anymore. I want him to move on and to let me move on as well. He is one of the biggest reasons I would consider leaving town, and, for a while there, he did suggest that I go, saying that I was cramping his style."

"His style, as in other relationships?"

"I don't know," she muttered, with a wave of her hand. "Of course everybody knows that we were once an item. Everybody knows most of the story—or at least they think they do. So I don't know how many people would hold that against him. He has a hold on a lot of things around here."

"Maybe not as much as you may think," he replied. "People's memories are not very long, so he shouldn't have a problem with moving on himself."

"Maybe not, but he is so ..." Shaking her head, she didn't even finish the statement.

Mateo had seen an awful lot of humanity, and it wasn't uncommon for someone to have an issue with their former partner moving on, and that didn't just apply to men. He'd seen plenty of women get jealous, not able to let go when their men moved on to other relationships. Mateo had seen it happen time and time again.

It wasn't exactly a great advertisement for relationships. He took a moment and thought about some of the people he knew who just couldn't move forward. Yet people like Badger and Kat helped him to see that not everybody was into this emotional blackmail scenario. His bosses had one of the best relationships he'd ever seen, and it gave him hope.

Hope for people in general, and hope for himself because there was just so much goodness in everything he saw in Badger and Kat.

He'd mentioned that to Kat at one point, and she had smiled and clarified, "Like everything, relationships take work, and it requires two people willing to do it. If that commitment isn't on both sides, it won't work. You cannot make up for another person if they're not interested in putting in the same amount of effort. At some point the other person just feels as if it's all on them, and they give up. It may not happen for ten years, or even twenty, but eventually they will walk away because they're depleted, having nothing left to give," she shared, "and you don't want to get into that scenario either."

They reached Maraya's house fairly quickly because they had moved faster on the return trip, just trying to get out of the cold. She immediately stomped her feet as she got to the front door. "For a while there I wasn't sure I would ever make it back," she muttered.

"Sorry. I shouldn't have taken you out on such a long trek."

She shook her head. "No, that had nothing to do with it. I'm more than happy to have gone. It just got cold so quick at the end that it caught me by surprise." She took off her gloves, then snatched up a thinner pair and announced, "I'll head in to the hospital."

He nodded. "I'll go as well."

She frowned at him and asked, "Do you want to come with me?"

He gave her a small smile. "Is that a good thing or a bad thing in terms of your ex? If I accompany you, is that okay, or will it just cause more trouble for you?"

She winced. "I'm not sure it's anything in particular. I just know that Riley's been difficult, no matter what."

"So, do you want him to think that you have another partner or just a friend?" he asked. "Or do you want to keep that appearance completely out of this issue?"

She stared at him and then started to laugh. "I hadn't even considered that. I don't care what he thinks."

"*You* may not, but it sounds as if he does. So it depends on whether you need or want that kind of an issue."

"I don't want *any* issues, but considering that we'll already be paired up because of finding the little boy, it'll be very hard to prevent people from talking or drawing conclusions."

"True, but we can also refer them to the War Department if you want a little more support and a little more camouflage or whatever. I'm not sure what to call it," he admitted, "but just the fact that you wouldn't be alone would give you a little more protection." She was about to protest, and he raised his hands. "Just something to consider."

"And that is ridiculous," she snapped.

He nodded. "I'm not arguing that, but I do recognize that you're not terribly happy that you have to go into the sheriff's domain. I'm not trying to do anything other than offer you a little support."

She groaned, pulled at her hair, while he watched the level of frustration she was going through.

"He really does set you off, doesn't he?"

She nodded. "In many ways he's not a nice man," she stated simply.

"In that case I'm going with you," he stated.

"One vehicle or two?"

He glanced at his watch. "Maybe two because I'll need to grab a motel and haven't even checked into that yet." He looked over at her and asked, "Do you have a recommendation?"

"Two are in town," she shared, "and both are okay, but, if you want, you could just stay here."

He stared at her steadily. "That might be pushing your comfort level more than you need to."

"Or," she countered, "it might also be helping me so I could sleep a little better tonight. It's unnerving to think that somebody was out there, trampling through the woods, then turned around and left a little boy out in the middle of nowhere."

He thought about that and nodded. "Have you got any idea what that was about?"

"No, I don't. Not one I want to contemplate at least, though I kind of suspect that you do."

His lips twitched. "I might have an idea," he noted, "but that doesn't mean I have answers. That would be a whole different story."

"Maybe, maybe not," she muttered, as she glared at him. "I suspect you've seen this stuff before."

"I've never seen anybody leave a child in the woods like that," he pointed out. "Either way, I do want to go to the hospital, and I do need a place to stay. If you have room for me, and I won't make you more uncomfortable than you already are, I would be happy to take you up on your offer." He was watching her closely for any reaction. What he saw was absolute relief. He nodded. "So that's settled then."

She smiled. "You're very perceptive."

He shrugged. "I've been in the world a long time, and I've seen some of the ugliness that people do to each other.

So, believe me when I say that I'm here to offer support if you want it, and I do not have a problem if you want to use it."

"Thank you," she muttered. "So, if you don't mind, we'll go into the station together tomorrow as well, and, if Riley doesn't like it, I'm certain we'll find out very quickly."

"Absolutely," Mateo agreed, "and, if he doesn't like it, we're always better off knowing that right up front."

She just nodded and didn't say a whole lot.

"How bad was it before?"

She stared at him, then sighed. "Bad enough."

"That's not an answer."

"No, and I'm not sure what to tell you. He was getting pretty damn scary. If I'd stayed, would he have hit me, beat me, or killed me? I don't think so. But what do I know? So, did he beat me? Technically, no. He did slap me too many times. Did I get out of there in time? Yes. Do I like being alone with him? No," she snapped. "I'm sorry. I shouldn't be taking it out on you."

"No, but I don't see anybody else here for you to take it out on," he added, with a note of humor.

She stared at him, and a reluctant grin crossed her face. "You really do handle this well, don't you?"

"Sometimes you have to handle things, even if you don't like it," he shared. "So, let's just get to the hospital, confirm Timmy is doing okay, and we'll carry on from there. And since I'm coming back here anyway, let's just take the one vehicle."

He watched from the front hall as she changed into a warmer jacket, grabbed her purse and keys, and walked back out again. He took one last look at the roomy, cozy, slightly old-looking home, very country and yet at the same time warm and filled with laughter. He smiled as he followed her to her vehicle. "You must have had a great relationship with your parents."

She looked at him and asked, "Why do you say that?"

"The house has that feel to it," he murmured, "friendly, warm, good memories."

"A lot of good memories," she confirmed, "and some that aren't so good, but again, you know, it's the devil you know." As she got into the driver's side, she looked over at him. "He could be at the hospital."

"Riley?" he asked, and she nodded. "Good. I'm not afraid of him, so let's go see how this little boy is."

"You might not be afraid of Riley, but he's—he's kind of scary."

"Yeah, well, what's scary to a young woman who has had some tough history with him, versus what's scary to somebody who's been all over the world fighting," he countered, "will be a very different thing, and believe me that Riley will know it immediately."

"Meaning that he's likely to be afraid of you?" she asked, and then she grinned. "Man, I would love to see that."

Mateo laughed. "I won't say that because I don't know just how used he's gotten to throwing his weight around town, but I don't think he will intimidate me."

"Let's go find out," she said. "Honest to God, it'll be interesting to get your take on him."

"Why is that?"

"Because apparently I don't have a very good grasp of him and the life that I had with him," she quipped. "According to him, I walked away from paradise."

"And according to you?"

"Hell in the making."

CHAPTER 5

M ARAYA COULDN'T BELIEVE how comfortable she was talking to Mateo. He was calm, not serene but just had this air of confidence about him, the sense of can-do versus can't-do. Something her father would have appreciated. Her mother was the kind of person to go off half-cocked at the first sign of trouble. She was somebody who panicked very, very quickly, whereas Mateo just looked at everything and made a nearly instantaneous decision that he would reserve judgment and go on from there.

It was a very strange thing, but one she appreciated. Her father, Henry Banks, used to tell her that it was their cross to bear when they were with somebody like her mother, who would immediately panic, and that it was up to them to try and make her world a little calmer and easier so she didn't react so violently to every outside influence. Maraya didn't quite understand what he meant until she was much older and realized that her mother had already been through some tough issues growing up, and that had made her very afraid of so much in life.

Her mother had spent the bulk of her adult years at home, working in the yard, just staying in the calmness of her own space. She had healed from whatever her earlier trauma had been, without ever giving too much clarification as to what that was. Over the years, her father would shake his head and say, "Don't ask."

But hearing that when you're a child just ignited a burning curiosity that made it very difficult to stay silent. Now, as an adult, Maraya realized it was none of her damn business, but that also didn't help because she wanted answers. She didn't know what had hounded her mother into being somebody who just couldn't handle any stress or any fast or difficult changes.

Not that anybody liked that or that anyone would want to adapt to something of that nature because it would mean they had more practice than anybody would really want. Still, Maraya found it hard to not know the details of what had happened to her mom. With both her parents gone now, it was even worse because Maraya didn't know if it was something relevant that she should know about, in terms of genetics or something like that. Yet her father had been pretty adamant about her not being told.

She had to admit a part of her had hoped there would be a death-bed letter, telling her what had gone on, but instead all she got was just that same enduring silence. So, whatever had happened, her father had been that security for her mother the entire lifetime they had spent together. There had been nobody else for either of them, and Maraya wanted that same kind of a marriage, but she surely didn't want to have whatever trauma Matilda Banks had gone through. Neither of her parents had been impressed with Maraya's getting pregnant, and they were even less impressed with the idea of her marrying Joseph.

At the time, she hadn't realized how bad things would get. The losses she'd experienced left her with a sense of not having any other avenue, and she'd ended up marrying Riley right away. She'd certainly had second thoughts along the line, but not a whole lot she could do about it at that point.

Her mother never told her that she shouldn't do it, but she had warned her that there was an awful lot more to marriage than having a roof over your head. The trouble was, her mother had never explained all the problems or issues with her own marriage or her history, so it was hard for Maraya to give too much credence to her mother's advice or lack thereof, given the situation.

Of course, everybody had been quietly disappointed in her pregnancy. Yet, because she was due to marry Joseph within weeks of finding out she was pregnant, many people would just turn a blind eye and smile because that's what hot young lovers were supposed to do—just not get caught.

When Joseph suddenly died, everything changed. She got the pitying looks, people shying away, and her mom would just sigh heavily all the time, and that hadn't helped either.

"Penny for your thoughts."

Mateo's voice startled her out of her reverie. She looked over at him and shrugged. "Just lots of long thoughts that don't do you any good."

"Ah, intrusive thoughts," he noted, looking out the windshield. "The ones that take you sideways, with no rhyme or reason. You think you're doing just fine, then, all of a sudden, this crap pops up, and you're wondering if maybe you're not so fine after all. It can be rough and … disorienting."

She frowned at him and slowly nodded. "It seems you understand."

That same grin popped out. "You might be surprised at what I understand," he stated. "I'm not here to do anything that would upset the apple cart. Yet I do need to know what happened to Thorny and what the future holds for him."

"Right," she muttered, "and that's a whole different story." Almost as if having heard his name, Thorny barked right behind her ear, making her wince.

Immediately Mateo turned and reached out a hand, and Thorny leaned heavily into it. "He's feeling pretty insecure himself," he muttered.

"Are you sure we should be bringing him to the hospital?"

"I'm sure. I don't know about the hospital administration," he noted, with a smile, "but, if the dog was a strong tie to the little boy, then it's important for both of them to reconnect."

"I don't know if he was for the little boy as much as he was for Donna, his sister. And maybe not even them. Emily mentioned that they wanted to get him so that Carlos could be comfortable around their home."

"Right, and then he came back different."

"Exactly, different enough that everybody was struggling with their new world."

"That's never an easy thing for anybody."

She just nodded as she pulled into the small hospital parking lot.

Mateo looked around, checking out the place. "Not very big, is it?"

"No, we have another bigger one about forty miles away."

He nodded. "Do we even know if Timmy is here?"

She winced. "We should have checked on that first, *huh*?"

"Yeah, but I didn't even think of it," he admitted. "We were focused on coming in."

"Right," she agreed, with a nod. She parked in the parking lot, looked over at him, and muttered, "For better or for worse."

He smiled and hopped out. "I think you might have gotten the phrase wrong. I think it was in sickness, in health, et cetera."

She snorted. "Yeah, Riley's vows were a little different than that, and I refused to say them too. It was one of the few times I bucked the entire family, and believe me that nobody appreciated it."

He burst out laughing. "No, if you buck the system, nobody wants you to do it in such a way that it shows you to be less than obedient."

"And *subservient*," she added, with some spirit. "I'd forgotten how much those things irritated me."

"Sounds as if your father put a strong sense of responsibility and independence into you."

"Henry Banks was a force. My mother, not so much, but my father was. I think that was part of the problem with the whole marriage thing. Dad didn't really approve of the Herman family, but, because I was pregnant, I'm not sure he felt he had any right to say anything about it."

"He could have told you that he would support you no matter what and that, although it might not be his choice for a life for you, as long as you were prepared to do your best to be a good mom and a strong independent woman, then you would think he would be there for you."

"You would think so," she noted, with a small smile. "They didn't make it much past that."

"Your parents? What happened to them?"

It took a moment for her to gather up enough energy to answer without breaking into tears. She turned to him.

"They died in a car accident, not far from here. It was one of the worst days of my life."

"It must have all happened very quickly," he said, looking at her steadily.

"Pregnancy, engagement, and then the car accident. My fiancé was in the car with my parents," she added, "which is why my entire world crashed. … My mom had asked Joseph and my dad to pick up a new fridge," she explained. "It would take two men, and Joseph was more than happy to help. So they were in the vehicle. My mother didn't go out much, but she went along to ensure it was the right fridge. She would only leave the house if my father was going. So, they all headed for town, and they were hit by a semi truck that had lost a tire and was out of control," she added. "A tire blew or something, and it suddenly careened sideways."

"Good God."

"Yeah, it was a tough time."

"And, just like that, his brother rushed you into marriage?"

"Yes, but I also let him rush me into marriage. I was numb to everything at that point in time." As she glanced back at Mateo, she realized his phraseology was quite true. "I guess it wasn't the right thing for Riley to do, but I think he was doing it more to keep me safe."

"And do you still think that now, even though you have a better idea of who he is?"

She stared at him. "That's not a question I had considered, and definitely not one I want to consider now." She hopped out of the vehicle and said, "Come on. Let's go see how Timmy is doing."

As they walked into the hospital, he glanced around and asked, "How well-known are you here?"

"In the hospital itself, not so much, but I've been in town all my life, so I know almost everybody here," she replied. "Any particular reason you are asking?"

He shrugged. "Just wondering how much people know about your relationships with the locals."

"As a teacher, I'm heavily involved with a lot of people."

"Right. So lots of connections to families?"

"Yes. … Why?"

"I'm just trying to get the lay of the land," he replied, with a smile. "It's not a problem."

"And yet somehow you make it sound as if there could be a problem."

He laughed. "Let's not look for issues where there aren't any."

"*Uh-huh.*" Walking through the entrance, they came upon a reception area. She smiled and called out, "Hi, Alex." The woman looked up, and a beaming smile immediately broke across her face.

"Hey. How are you doing, Maraya?"

"We came to check on Timmy, the little boy we found."

Surprise lit her face. "You found him?"

"We did, but why the face?"

"That's not what the sheriff said."

"Of course not," Maraya muttered in a dry tone, "but the two of us found him."

At that, her gaze went to the man beside her and back again. Alex frowned. "Riley said that his men found him."

"That's nice," Mateo noted in a dry tone, "but it wasn't him, and it wasn't his men."

Still frowning, Alex kept looking from one to the other, as if seeking more information.

Calmly Mateo asked, "What room is the little boy in?"

Alex shook her head. "I'm sorry, but only family is allowed."

"Really?" he asked. "So, the people who found him and rescued him don't get to see him?"

"I would have to talk to the doctor," Alex noted apologetically.

"Good. Who's on call tonight?" Maraya asked.

Alex looked over at her and replied, "Dr. Wilson."

"Perfect, call him for me, please," she asked cheerfully. Soon she realized they wouldn't even have to, when a man called out from the other side.

"Hey, Maraya. How are you doing?"

She turned and saw the old doctor, one who she had been seeing since she was very small. "Hey, Dr. Wilson. How are you?"

"I'm fine. Are you here to see somebody?" he asked curiously. "You're not injured, are you, or sick?"

"Nope, I'm just fine," she replied, a smile on her face. "We came to see the little boy we rescued from the woods today."

His eyebrows shot up. "You rescued him?"

She nodded. "Mateo and I did."

He looked at Mateo, then back at her.

"I understand from Alex here that my dear ex-husband may have put out a different story."

Dr. Wilson flushed and nodded. "According to him, Rodney and Xavier found Timmy."

"Interesting," she noted, "since they could barely even be bothered to search for the missing family from the beginning, much less help us look earlier for any of the other family members who have been missing all this time too."

"What? Are you saying more people are missing?" he asked.

She stared at him. "I'm sure you've realized by now that Timmy's entire family disappeared off the face of the earth about ten days ago," she shared. "I've been trying to get somebody to listen, but everything I've said seems to have fallen on deaf ears."

"So, how did you find Timmy?"

"We heard a dog barking and knew Carlos's family had a War Dog, also missing. So we followed the barking. Then we found Timmy with nobody else around, just the dog," she shared, as she pointed down at Thorny at her side. "And, no, the deputies wouldn't even go out and see if the rest of the family is out there even now."

He just stared at her in confusion. "Why wouldn't they do that?" he asked.

"No idea," she replied. "We just came back from a long trek out in the backwoods, but we didn't find the rest of the family. I'm tired. I'm cold, and I just want to ensure that Timmy is doing okay."

"He's doing fine. I can tell you that much."

"We would sure like to see him," she stated firmly. "We worked hard to bring him back, and I want to see with my own eyes that he is here and that he's okay. I would like to sleep tonight and to not have nightmares about little children stuck out in the middle of nowhere by some asshole who dumped them there."

He just stared at her for a long moment. "I'm sorry, but you're not family."

"Right, and, for all we know, Timmy's entire family is dead," she snapped. "And again we're the ones who brought him in. Are you telling me that we can't even take a look to ensure that he's here? And that he's okay?"

He hesitated, and she turned to Mateo.

He had one eyebrow raised as he watched the doctor with a narrow gaze. "I'm not sure why that would be a problem," he added in a polite tone. "It would seem to be a natural wish on our part to confirm that the little boy is okay."

"I can certainly assure you that we're doing everything we can for him," the doctor replied, "but you aren't family."

"So, just who is it you're allowing in to comfort the boy? It's important to have that little boy know that his dog, who was standing guard over him, is okay, and I very much need for Thorny here to see that the little boy is okay as well."

At that, Dr. Wilson stared down at the dog and frowned.

Mateo added, "I'm sensing that you're about to tell me how that's a problem as well."

"He's not a therapy dog," he pointed out instantly. "He doesn't have any credentials to be here, so it's not exactly an easy thing for me to just overturn hospital rules."

"Overturn hospital rules," Maraya repeated in a very soft tone.

Dr. Wilson flushed again. "I mean, obviously we're doing everything we can for the little boy."

"You haven't even given me a condition update," she said. "You just tell me that he's here and that he's doing fine, and that doesn't tell me anything at all."

"He's doing fine, though he's not awake yet," he added, "and that is something we're concerned about."

"I would think so," Mateo grumbled. He pulled out his phone and quickly sent off a series of texts.

She had no idea who he was contacting and just ignored it while she focused on the doctor. "So, you're telling me that I can't even look through the window myself to ensure that he's here so I can sleep tonight?" Again the doctor hesitated, and she reached out a hand. "Please, I just want to know he's okay. One look is all I need."

"I don't know why you won't just take my word for it," he muttered, throwing up his hands, "but fine, you can come see, but you can't go in." He immediately turned on his heels and stalked down the hallway.

She followed, dragging Mateo with her. "You really need to pay attention here."

"Oh, I am," he replied. "I'm just working on getting a little more pull added to my visit here."

She stared at him. "I have no idea what that means, but, if it'll help us do what we need to do, it's a good thing."

"It is definitely a good thing," he declared, with a smile. "Remember that I'm not just here on a whim."

She brightened at that. "Right, so by rights, we should get in to see Timmy."

"It'll take a little bit of effort to make that happen—maybe," he shared, "but I'm hopeful that we can at least get upgrades and some special treatment for the little guy."

They were led to a private room, where they could stand at the doorway. As she peered in the window of the door, she saw Timmy lying motionless in a bed. "Oh, good God," she said, her hand going to her cheek.

"He's doing fine," Dr. Wilson repeated. "And I understand how concerned you must be if you found him out there on your own."

"There's no *if* about it," Mateo corrected, shooting him a glance.

"And, of course, you can prove that, right?" the doctor asked, eyeing him intently.

Mateo stared at him. "You're telling me the 9-1-1 call

that Maraya made wasn't enough? You're telling me that I have to prove that we were the ones who found the dog so the kudos don't go to your sheriff's department? Is that how this county works?"

Dr. Wilson flushed once more. "All I know is what I've been told. It doesn't matter to me either way. I just was hoping for more information from whoever found him. The deputies couldn't give me much."

"Yeah, that's because they weren't there," Mateo declared. "Now, what is it you want to know?"

"Did he have any extra clothing with him? Did he have anything to identify where he had been? Is that the boy at all?"

Mateo stared at the doctor. "You do realize his teacher is standing right beside you, and she has confirmed the boy is Timmy from the same family who abruptly disappeared. The very same ones she just told you about."

He glanced over at her and nodded. "I know that. I'm just telling you that some people aren't willing to take that at face value."

Confused, Mateo stared at the doc, not getting the issue at all. "Aren't you willing to take Maraya's word for something so obvious? What is really going on here?"

"There appears to be some discrepancies as to why or how the little boy may have gone missing."

Not sure exactly what was going on, Mateo asked, "What does that even mean? Are you implying that Maraya had something to do with it?"

"Well, it is a well-known fact—but maybe not for you. You may not know her history."

"And maybe I do," he responded, staring at him with a narrowed gaze. "But please, fill me in." Just then he saw the look on her face, and he knew that things were about to get interesting.

She turned and looked at the doctor, and she was furious. "Seriously? Are you thinking I took the little boy and then, when he came down with whatever is wrong with him right now, I sent him to the hospital with some cock-and-bull story about having found him out in the woods?" She was red in the face and glaring daggers at this man she had known her whole life. If looks could kill, she was lethal at the moment.

Dr. Wilson immediately shook his head. "No, no, no, we aren't saying that, but I can tell you that the deputy did say that they found him."

"I don't care what the deputy *said*," she cried out, "because that is a ridiculous lie."

"Which is also why I don't understand why they would say that," he replied, looking at her intently.

"Versus what I am saying, you mean?"

He shrugged. "I don't know why they would. I mean, they are law enforcement."

"And what am I?" she asked, staring at the doctor in disbelief. "Good God, you've known me for how long? How can you—"

"Of course, but I also know—" Then he stopped.

"You also know my history with children," she snapped, glaring at him. "And you think that I might have done something, or in some way needed to boost myself up by creating a story about a little boy because I miss my own. Is that it?"

He flushed all shades of red and then abruptly added, "I have to get back to work." And, with that, he quickly escaped down the hall.

She stared at Mateo, numb. "In all my life," she whispered, "it never occurred to me that anybody would see me in such a light."

"I highly suspect," Mateo murmured, "that somebody has been smearing your mental stability."

"In which case," she snapped, "everything I worked so hard to earn—like hopefully getting back to my career in the future—is on the line, and that is not a good thing. Because no way they'll have anybody with any instability, real or imagined, working in the school."

"Is there any chance that Riley's trying to either push you away or to pull you closer to him?"

"I don't care what he's trying to do," she murmured, "but I can tell you that it won't work." She scrubbed her face and took a deep breath. "I can't believe what I'm hearing."

"Neither can I," Mateo agreed, and just then his phone buzzed. He smiled at her and said, "Hang on." He took a few steps away and checked his texts on his phone.

She watched him scrolling on his phone, his expressions going from one of surprise to a narrowed gaze as he read on, and then a small grin appeared.

He looked back at her and nodded. "It's all right. Things will be fine."

"Why is that?"

"Because I had texted Badger earlier how we had found the little boy, remember?"

"Sure."

"They were tracking us on satellite, the two of us, not the damn deputies."

She looked up at him, confusion in her eyes. "What does that mean?"

"I would hate to even bring it up, but what it means is,

we have concrete proof that we found Timmy."

AS MATEO WATCHED the joy and relief cross her face, he absolutely hated that anybody would have tried to cause this situation for her. "I don't know what's going on," he stated, "but we need to get to the bottom of it." Just watching Maraya's joy, pain, and hurt caused by hearing the doctor's lies was something else. Mateo glanced back down at his phone and quickly sent Badger a message, with an update on the doctor's words.

When Badger phoned him, he stepped away from her for a moment, excusing himself. "Just let me take this." He walked down the hallway a little bit. "Badger, I don't have a clue what's going on here, but I've never seen anything like it."

"You're telling me the sheriff said that the deputies found the little boy?"

"Yeah. Maybe they don't have any good PR, so they stole that from her and from me," he suggested, with a laugh. "Not that I care."

"You might not care, but I do," Badger declared in his brutally honest way. "And that is something I'll be checking into a little further."

"And yet they were just probably trying to make their department look better."

"Sure," Badger noted, "that may be, but trying to make someone else look worse in order to make themselves look better is a new low. Not many people can do that."

"There is some relevant background," Mateo added, then he quickly shared the information on her relationship with the sheriff, as well as the accident that killed her parents and fiancé and her subsequent miscarriage.

Badger was incredibly touched that she was even doing as well as she was. "That's got to be hard. It's bad enough to deal with any one of those events, but to have them all happen so close together is brutal."

"That's what I was thinking, but she is doing okay."

"I'll do a quick check into the town and whatnot, and I"—he chuckled—"I have an idea or two. I'll run them past Kat and see what she thinks."

"What do you want me to do in the meantime?"

"What do you want to do?"

"Stick by her, check to see if we can find the missing family."

"Stay in touch. I'm glad you got the dog, and we do need to figure out where he'll reside from here on out," Badger reminded him. "That is a concern still."

"I know, but I don't want to make any plans if the rest of the family is out there. Like who the hell does that with a little child?"

"You and I both know stranger things have happened. Unfortunately we just don't like what the answers are likely to be."

"I know, and I haven't brought that up to her either."

"You may not want to just yet," he forewarned. "Let's get a few more things in place first."

Mateo rang off and turned to walk back to her, standing there, the fatigue more evident on her face now, her shoulders slumped as she stared at the little boy. "At least he's here where he belongs."

She looked up, gave him a little smile, and nodded. "Remember when you were asking me about leaving town earlier?" He nodded. "After today, I'm thinking that's exactly what I need to do. It's been pretty rough at times, but shit's really hitting the fan now."

"Yeah, it sounds like it. Come on." He motioned her to move. "Let's get you home so you can get some rest."

She sighed. "You would make a great caregiver, you know?"

He winced at that. "Not exactly something I ever expected to get a compliment for," he said, with half a laugh.

She shrugged. "I think caregivers get very little joy in life. Everybody just seems to think that you're there to do a job, and you rarely get thanked for it."

"Sounds as if you have been there."

"Sure. After my parents died, I had only my aunt, and she had cancer. I had already lost them all—my parents and Joseph, then our baby. After that, I ended up spending a lot of time with her. That was a pretty rough deal too."

"Good God." Mateo stared at her. "Sounds as if you've only had death and loss in your life these last many years."

She nodded. "Maybe that's why I focus so much on the children, and why these ones in particular, this family disappearing hurts so much. There was no need for them to just disappear like that," she exclaimed. "Not only no need, there's no reasonable explanation, but nobody seems to care."

"I'm not sure that nobody cares," he clarified, "as much as … the potential circumstances don't leave behind any real clues."

"Whatever the excuse," she said, looking at him, "I haven't gotten any answers."

"And maybe the authorities haven't found any either."

"And I can see why," she declared. "Did you see how

much effort they put in today?"

He winced at that and nodded. "I brought that up with my boss too."

"Good, maybe he has more pull in getting a full search of the area."

"Maybe, maybe not—or maybe it would be something I end up doing quietly on the side."

She frowned at him. "Is that something you're trained for?"

He grinned. "Absolutely. Don't you worry about that."

She shrugged. "As long as you're okay with it. I don't want to dump all these problems on you just because you're here."

"They're here, and they're connected to my War Dog assignment," he stated, as he stroked Thorny. "Let's get him home. Do you have any dog food by chance?"

She frowned and shook her head. "No, and he's got to be starving." She looked down at the dog who was looking pretty damn tired too. "Look at him. We need to get him home."

"Yes, we do." And they headed back out to her car.

"We have a grocery store here that's open late," she shared, pointing to the area. "They should have some dog food." They did a quick trip inside, and he managed to pick up a couple small bags of dry food. As soon as they got back to her place, she handed him a regular dish and suggested, "Maybe you can make that work."

He quickly fed the War Dog, and Thorny dug in with gusto, as if he'd been waiting all day to be fed, though maybe he'd been waiting way longer than that. Mateo watched the ferocity with which he ate and sent a quick text back to Badger, explaining how hungry the dog had been.

He got a thumbs-up in response, and he turned to find Maraya in the kitchen, looking in the fridge. "I guess we should have picked up some food," he added, "for us, not just the dog."

She nodded. "If I'd thought that far ahead, I would have mentioned it. I'm sorry. I guess it goes to show just how tired I am. I'm standing here, like an idiot, staring into the fridge, as if somehow expecting it to give me more food."

"Are you hungry?"

She considered it and then shrugged. "I think I'm too-far-past hungry. I'm just so tired now that I can't even think straight."

"Have you got any eggs in there?" After she reported having both eggs and cheese, she named a few other potential ingredients she had on hand. "Perfect," he declared, "Let me whip up a quick omelet, and then we can both crash."

She closed the fridge door, a stunned expression on her face. "Don't tell me that you cook too?"

He snorted. "Any guy who's been single for very long knows how to cook simple things like an omelet," he stated, with a smile. "It's really not difficult."

"I know it's not difficult," she replied. "I'm just not used to anybody stepping up and doing it."

"I've been cooking for myself for a long time, and, if you have a barbecue, I could make you a mean steak."

"And I would definitely let you," she agreed, looking at him.

"Good." He checked the cabinets for what he needed. "We'll pick up some steaks tomorrow."

She laughed, and then a serious thought interrupted. "How long do you think you'll be here?"

He turned to her and added, "If my being here is an issue, you just tell me, and I'll go get a place to stay in town."

"No, no, no," she countered, shaking her head. "I'm not worried about that at all. I'm wondering if you'll be okay here. It's not as if I have a restaurant around the corner where you can go get food."

He waved his hand. "Doesn't matter if you did or not," he replied, his tone casual. "I'm quite happy to cook. It's just a matter of having stuff on hand. So, one way or another, we'll make a trip tomorrow to pick up some groceries."

She smiled at that. "I would never say no to that. I am so ready for bed, but I think you're right. I'll be better off getting some food first."

"Absolutely, so just give me a couple minutes." He looked at her, with her hair all messed up and her clothes dirty. "Do you want a hot shower while I cook, or would you rather eat first? It will be done in no time."

She laughed. "I would be happy to eat now and then go up and shower, if you can do it that fast." And then she frowned and added, "Jesus, listen to me." She chuckled. "There's absolutely no reason I can't make an omelet."

He immediately stepped forward and took the pan she'd grabbed. "It's fine. Just sit down. How about a cup of tea or something?"

She nodded. "Tea sounds absolutely wonderful."

He quickly put on the kettle, found the items in the fridge that he wanted, and within minutes had an omelet going. He looked back at her and asked, "Do you lock your doors at night?"

She shook her head. "Not really, it's not that kind of town. Why?"

"I'm just thinking—now that we have Thorny with us— maybe we should."

"Do you think he'll go out at night?"

"He might if he had a reason, but he can't open the door. However, if anybody would open the door, we could lose him."

"Oh, we won't have that happen." Then she frowned and added, "I really don't like the inference that somebody might open the door either."

He gave her a gentle smile. "I was hoping you were too tired to notice."

"You're thinking about whoever or whatever Thorny saw out there."

"I am, and I noticed you didn't mention it to the doctor."

"No, and I likely won't mention it to the sheriff tomorrow either."

"Why is that?" he asked curiously.

"Because I'm not sure that he gives a crap, and, if we'll have trouble, I would just as soon know what kind of trouble we're in for."

"Right."

Just then she yawned, and the teakettle went off at the same time.

He laughed. "Sit tight. The eggs are cooking, and let's get you a cup of tea, and you'll be eating very soon. I promise." And he was true to his word, as they were sitting down and eating within just a few minutes.

She stared at the omelet, and it looked delicious. "Honest to God, it looks amazing. It smells amazing. I'm just hungry enough to not appreciate it."

"Nothing to appreciate," he said. "It's food. It's hot, and it's necessary for our system, so dig in. Then you can get to bed."

She groaned. "I'll take you up on that offer. I think I might even pass on the shower and get one in the morning," she shared, scrubbing her face. "The cold seems to have gotten into my soul, and it's so hard to warm up."

"That's a large part of it. It's partly fatigue, partly the effects of the adrenaline, the excitement of finding Timmy, yet not finding the rest of the family. It's all kinds of stuff," he noted. "However, it's all good because we did find one of them. It's progress. He's in the hospital and getting care, and that's very important."

She gave him a quiet smile. "Yes, it's unbelievable how good that is. We just need to keep looking for the rest of his family."

"And yet why would he turn up and not the rest of his family?" Mateo asked almost to himself. "That's the part I don't get. We got Timmy, but there's no sign of the rest of them."

"No, I don't get it either," she muttered, "unless—"

He looked over at her, one eyebrow raised, and she shrugged. "You're thinking what I'm thinking, I suppose?" he asked.

She looked at him and sighed. "I don't know. You tell me."

"Unless whoever took the family realized the little boy was sick, heard us, and left the boy out where he was, hoping we would find him. He would have left the dog to protect the boy, to ensure no animals got him, and, as it turned out, Thorny's barking led us out there, so we could find both of them."

She looked at him and slowly nodded. "I did have some wild variations of that in my head," she admitted, "but I still don't know why anybody would do that."

"I don't know either, but it also means," he added, taking a deep breath, "that we're being watched, and the whole time we were out there, somebody was following us and was keeping track."

"That's the part I really don't like," she declared, staring at him as a shiver ran down her spine. "That's a really horrible thought."

"I don't know how horrible it is," he said, brushing it off, "but it's definitely something we have to consider. We have a lot of unknowns right now, and I'm not sure just exactly what's going on, but the good news is, we have Timmy, and we have Thorny."

"The bad news is," she interjected, pointing her fork at him, "a mother, a father, and a little girl are still missing."

"And I haven't forgotten that," he stated, "but let's take the wins we have, get some sleep, and come back fighting tomorrow."

CHAPTER 6

MARAYA WOKE THE next morning, rolled over, and immediately moaned. Her body was sore and stiff, as if she'd gone for a ten-mile hike. As she thought about it, she realized she probably had. It was amazing to note just how out of shape she was. Yesterday's trample through the woods looking for Thorny, then Timmy, then anybody else out there, had come with unexpected consequences. The bitter nighttime cold hadn't helped either.

She shifted out of bed and immediately headed to the shower. As soon as she stood under the hot water, some of the stress and pain eased, and it didn't take very long to start feeling like a whole new person again. Soon she was back in her room getting dressed and bustling downstairs, hoping to get coffee on before Mateo woke up. And yet, as she walked into the kitchen, there he sat, on his phone, sipping a cup of coffee.

He looked up and smiled. "Hey, you look great."

"I look great?" she repeated.

"Yeah, way better than last night."

"Oh good," she muttered, checking out her reflection in the glass of a cupboard door. "In that case, I must have been a real vision last night."

He chuckled at that. "You were exhausted, worn out, and quite stressed from it all. The adrenaline rush had ended, and you were pulling on your reserves," he pointed out. "So don't feel bad about whatever shape you were in last night. You were still standing, and that in itself was pretty impressive."

"Thank you."

"And I hope you don't mind, but I found the coffee."

She laughed. "I was planning on getting down here to put some coffee on before you woke up, but look at you. You've already got it ready."

"Well, I'm partial to coffee."

She nodded. "Me too," she murmured, with a smile.

"In that case, let me get you a cup." He hopped up, and, before she had a chance to say anything or to even move, he had already poured her a cup and set it down in front of her. "Now you can sit down and relax."

She looked at the cup on the table and slowly sank down as she stared at it. "You know, not to make a big thing out of this," she began, "but I really can't remember the last time anybody made a simple cup of coffee for me."

He smiled. "My pleasure. Now, I've also been in touch with my boss this morning," he stated, eyeing her closely, "and it seems a few of the things that you mentioned might not be true."

She froze, frowned at him, and muttered, "Pardon?"

He hesitated. "Apparently you are not a teacher right now."

"I told you that I'm working at the dentist's office. However, yes, I am still a teacher but just not working at the school right now," she clarified, feeling a sense of betrayal and the inevitable dread of facing something she didn't want to deal with. "Although that seems to be an issue for you."

"And why is that?" he asked, staring at her, something

odd in his gaze.

It wasn't an accusation, more of a quest for the truth. "Because I was considered to *not* be the desirable type for the school, but I did just get my job back after quite a fight, mostly because they don't have any teachers. Yet I will add with certainty that they will be looking for a way to get rid of me again."

"And can you explain what you did that they didn't like?"

"Yeah, it's very simple. I got divorced," she snapped, glaring at him. "You didn't have to do an investigation on me, you know? All you have to do is ask me."

"Yes, but my boss went the extra mile, mostly because of the town's attitude toward you, even though you're involved with finding Timmy. Badger is a very thorough guy, and he wanted to ensure that everything in your world is okay and won't be messed up by what the sheriff did."

"Since the sheriff is the one who also told everybody that I was having an affair, giving him full justification for divorcing me as an unfit woman," she added, with a head-shake of disgust, "he managed to slur my name pretty good."

"And is that why you were questioned over your job?"

"You mean, is that why I lost my job?" she asked. Mateo nodded. "Yes," she stated, her tone bitter, "at least I think that was part of it. It was a bit of a mess. If I didn't have this property here and hadn't lived here all my life, I probably would have left a long time ago."

"He also managed to have you committed."

She groaned, closed her eyes, and sank back in her chair. "Wow, your boss really is thorough."

"Yes, he is."

"So, yes, Riley managed to get me sectioned for a few

days because he told everybody how I was suicidal and how I wasn't stable. That's the other reason my suitability as a teacher was called into question. I was given a six-month leave of absence and was only recently notified that I'll soon be allowed back to work."

"I'm sorry. … So that's why you've been working for the dentist then."

She waved her hand as she nodded. "I would like to think that I can deal with this crap, and it's over," she shared. "I was found completely sane and normal, by the way. Yet still the whole ugly thing is now forever documented, and, thanks to my lovely ex, anyone can find those records," she noted. "I don't even know if I could get a job somewhere else because, once that pops up, even if they think you're okay, they wouldn't want the liability. I'm supposed to go back to school here pretty soon, but I don't know if the families will be happy about it."

"And that's why the doctor at the hospital was eyeing you with such concern."

She stared at him and then nodded. "You are very sharp," she finally said. "I was hoping nobody would notice."

"I don't know that he meant it in the wrong way, but is he the one who sectioned you?"

"No, that was a friend of Riley's, a family doctor who's also been around here a long time. Unfortunately he's also ancient, and he took my husband's words that I was suicidal."

"And were you?"

"No," she snapped sharply, "if I ever were so inclined to do something like that, I would have done it after I lost my parents and my fiancé." She pointed a finger at him. "And, yes, I was still pregnant at that time. Would I have done something back then if I wasn't pregnant? No. I don't think so, but I don't know. At any rate, I wasn't in good shape at that point in time. If I had been, I never would have married Riley in the first place."

"Of course not," he murmured. "I'm sorry that you've had quite the runaround."

"And yet it feels very much as if Riley's still making my life hell."

"It definitely sounds like he is. I mean, you weren't even given credit for having found the kid."

"And yet I wouldn't have found him if it wasn't for you," she added, "so you're the one who is getting railroaded."

He laughed. "I don't care, but my boss? He's not having it." He pulled out his phone, clicked through, and then passed it to her. "This is hitting the headline news this morning."

She took the phone from him and read the article he had brought up for her. "Oh my God," she muttered, staring at it. "That's both you and I there, confirmed by a satellite image."

"Yep, and we didn't release this to the press, so it's got nothing to do with us," he stated, with a laugh. "Not that your ex will particularly appreciate this, but the credit has been given directly to us."

She shook her head. "Man, I might need to leave town sooner than I thought," she said, a touch of panic in her tone. "Riley won't take that well."

"Sorry. I had no clue Badger would do this, but he really hates injustice, and so does his wife."

"That is just too much though," she said, staring at him. "Riley and his deputies won't like it."

"They might not like it, but they're the liars in the first place, and they've been called out in a big way. So, unless they would care to explain the *confusion* to the media," he noted, "they will likely just drop it. By the way, I also have permission to take Thorny into the hospital whether the personnel like it or not."

She sat back and stared at him, her jaw dropping slightly. "Wow, your bosses have more pull than anybody I know."

"They're also very connected in the medical world, and anything that would help that little boy, particularly a War Dog that would stand guard over Timmy, is considered to be good for his mental health."

"Right," she agreed, yet with a headshake. "I am not at all sure how the hospital will handle that."

"That's their issue. Memos have already been issued to the hospital from the board of directors."

"Well, that should be fun," she muttered, "because I can't imagine anybody there backing down either."

"And it's likely to make me even more unpopular," he stated, with a smile, "because nobody likes having their toes stepped on."

"Of course not," she agreed, "but I'm kind of enjoying this. I mean, if you'll step on toes, you might as well choose some big ones, so they're worthy enough to stomp."

He laughed.

"So, what will you do this morning?" she asked, as she sipped her coffee, which he'd done a bang-up job on too. It seemed as if there wasn't anything this guy couldn't do.

"I'm heading back out," he announced. Then turning toward her, he added, "Before you ask, I'll just say it. You're not coming with me."

She rolled her eyes. "I was tired last night and a little sore this morning, but I'm not that bad."

"I want you to stay here and to run interference, if need be."

She cocked her head and asked, "Do you think anybody is coming?"

"We have a ground crew coming to explore with me," he shared. "After yesterday, Badger didn't want me going out there alone, especially since, if something happened to me, you would be on your own until Badger was alerted."

She just stared at him.

"So, some friends are close by," he added casually. "I wasn't even thinking they were around here, but apparently my boss has a couple guys he's worked with multiple times nearby. They're on their way and expected in soon. So, we'll do a full check back there, where we found Timmy."

"Good," she said, feeling a sense of relief. "And you are sure these guys are okay?"

"Yeah, they've worked with Badger before, so I'm sure it's fine," he replied. "I don't even know who it is yet, but it's possible I know them."

"That's good," she noted, "because, as you know, nobody here seemed to really give a crap."

"I'm not sure whether it's a lack of local support or just a lack of awareness," he offered, shaking his head. "I don't want to blame everybody in town if it's really because law enforcement isn't rising to the occasion. Maybe they're just ill-equipped or poorly trained. Sometimes people just won't have the time, energy, or knowledge to even go searching for lost people."

"Maybe," she muttered, "but it does seem as if they could have done *something*."

"Exactly, which is why these two guys are coming."

"So, the three of you are heading out, and I'm supposed to do what?"

"Stay here and don't let anybody else come out after us, if the deputies show up."

"I won't be able to stop them, and you already know that."

"Maybe," he agreed, "but, if anybody does come, if anybody shows up in any capacity, including your ex, you tell me."

"We're also supposed to go give our statements."

"Yes, we are," he confirmed, "and we can do that when we get back."

"How long do you expect to be?"

"I suspect we'll be a few hours, but, once that is accomplished, you and I can head into town and give our statements."

"And these men?"

He smiled. "I suspect that, if we don't find anything, they'll probably keep on looking. It depends on who all is around."

"And you don't know if you know these guys?"

"I don't know at the moment, but I asked Badger to send me names when he had it finalized," he shared, pulling his phone toward him again and checking his messages. "I suspect I probably know them. As I mentioned before, I was building homes for vets with a lot of Badger's guys. Plus, many of us served together at one time or another too."

She smiled. "Building the houses is pretty amazing."

"It is," he agreed, "though it can also be frustrating. Everything has to be adapted to wheelchairs and other equipment that goes along with the physical needs of the individual. ... Often we're dealing with people who are still working through things and are emotionally attached to what they lost. It can all make for both heart-warming and heart-wrenching experiences."

"And when you say, *what they lost,* what do you mean exactly?" she asked.

"Some of them come back to find wives gone, children moved on. Some of them were ditched while still overseas. Some of them come back minus body parts or with traumatic brain injuries. It's very difficult for the veteran and their families, and sometimes it just doesn't go that well," he explained. "Believe me that it's quite an adjustment."

She winced and nodded. "God, but how rewarding for you to provide them with houses."

"Sometimes, and sometimes very frustrating too," he admitted, with a smile. "We're always looking for money to keep it going. Badger didn't intend to get into this area, but he's got a big team of men with him, and somehow they've ended up with this business that all of them are working on, and it's really important to everyone."

"Of course it is."

"He has a lot of other military contacts and groups that he taps for money when he needs to, but, for the most part, we do what we can as efficiently as possible. Still, there's never enough money. Last I knew, he had sixteen more homes in line to build immediately," he noted. "And why shouldn't they have homes? They've worked damn hard for our country, and they've paid a huge price. In many cases, it doesn't matter how many surgeries, how much physical therapy, or how much counseling they get, there's still very little anybody can do for them. So, we do what we can, and we give them a home and a life that comes with them afterward."

She smiled. "For all that tough-guy exterior of yours, you're just a big teddy bear inside."

His eyes widened, then he grinned, leaned forward, and whispered, "Don't tell anybody."

She burst out laughing, then heard a vehicle out front. The look on her face got him as he gripped her hand and reminded her, "It'll be my guys."

She sagged back in her chair and shook her head. "Why am I terrified all of a sudden?"

"Because so much shit is going on right now, and you've been living for too long under a constant strain from that ass of an ex," he pointed out, trying to ease her mind. "So, we'll have to find a way to fix that, but first let's see if anybody is outside." He asked her, "Are you okay if I take these guys and go?"

She immediately nodded. "Yes. I know you need to, and it's the right thing to do."

"It is the right thing to do, but I don't really want to leave you alone, if you're not comfortable with it."

She laughed. "I've been alone for a long time—or at least it feels like it. I'll be fine. Go find everyone else, find what happened to that family. And then at least I can leave this town with a full heart, knowing that I did what I could."

"Sounds good." He got up, walked to the front door, opened it, and stepped out.

She immediately raced behind him, not sure if he would bring the guys in or what, but, as she stepped outside, she saw two men, one with a prosthetic leg that he wasn't covering up at all, and why should he? He certainly shouldn't have to, but a lot of people would be uncomfortable looking at it. She called out to them, "Good morning. There is coffee if you want a cup before you leave."

Both men turned to her and smiled. "Thanks, ma'am, but we'll head out, and hopefully we can come back with some answers."

They looked back at Mateo, who waved at her and added, "We'll drive this time and head up on a different pathway, get a little bit closer from the other side."

She nodded. "I didn't even think about that, but I guess we were so far that it probably is closer from the other side."

"It might be. I'll stay in touch." And, with that, he got into the vehicle with Thorny and the two men, and they drove away.

She stared after them, still holding her empty coffee cup. Slowly she headed back inside and sat down on a chair, wondering at how her world had suddenly changed.

Just as she was pouring a second cup of coffee, her phone rang. She glanced down and noted it was Riley. She hesitated, not sure if she should answer it or not, and waited for the answering machine to pick it up.

As soon as she heard his angry voice, she was glad she hadn't taken that call.

"Pick up the damn phone. What the hell are you doing, handing out articles and getting yourself on front page news? What the hell do you think this is?"

She stared at the phone, and then she started to laugh because she hadn't done anything, but he would blame her for it, as he blamed her for everything anyway. She sat and listened to the rest of it.

"You better get your ass down here and get those statements in, and I want to have a talk with you about stealing the thunder from my boys. I ain't taking that shit, so you'll print a retraction immediately." And, with that, he ended the call.

Only she hadn't posted the article and didn't have a clue who or what or why. It wasn't anything she was in any position to change, but he was obviously pissed, and she was sorry that Mateo was gone, but he wasn't fully gone.

She picked up her phone and quickly sent him a text with the gist of Riley's message. Mateo's response was same as always, calm and reassuring.

Of course he's mad. He lost his thunder, but we didn't have anything to do with it. So, not to worry. I'll pass the message on to Badger, and we'll let Riley stew for a while, before he finds out who else might have posted that article.

She sent him a text back. **He will be a problem, and he won't be easy to handle.**

You didn't do it, so try to relax if you can. We'll be in touch soon.

His response was short, but he was right. She needed to let him handle whatever this was. And, with that, she finished her coffee and headed back upstairs to crash for a little bit longer. Even if just to rest and to get some peace, she could use a little more time to herself this morning. But she couldn't help grinning at the thought of the outrage that Riley must have felt when he saw the article, scooping the credit for Timmy's rescue right out from under him.

As a matter of fact, it might keep her in smiles right throughout the day.

MATEO SAT IN the truck mapping out the place where they'd found the boy and planning where they'd look today. He had insisted on bringing Thorny with him. The other men had taken to Thorny instantly, and the War Dog was in his element once again, doing lots of the work he had done in the military.

"He's a hell of a dog," Jacks stated.

"I know." Mateo smiled. "He's pretty special. I've been wondering about him, ever since he showed up."

"*Huh*, that's what Badger does," he pointed out, with a smile. "I mean, he gets you all hooked on these dogs, and then you want one for your own, and you pretty well make a fool out of yourself until you get it."

"I'm not sure anything's wrong with that either," Mateo quipped, as he smiled at Jacob. "Thanks for coming out and giving me a hand with this."

"Not an issue," they both replied immediately.

"Badger was telling us about some of the crap that's been going on here," Jacob shared. "We see it way too often, and it still pisses us off."

Jacks looked back at Mateo and asked, "Will you head up that new building project?"

"It's on my mind, yeah. I was talking to Badger about it, when Kat tagged me for this job."

Jacks laughed. "It seems she's really good at that. She's also got this matchmaking thing going on."

Mateo snorted. "No matchmaking in my world. I'm doing good, but I'm not quite ready for that."

"Oh, I don't know," Jacks countered, followed by a booming laugh. "I'm surprised you didn't kiss that pretty little lady goodbye when we left this morning."

"I just met her yesterday," he pointed out, shaking his head at them. But they both had big grins on their faces, and he knew they meant no harm.

Jacks added, "If Kat ever gets an idea that you might be sweet on Maraya, you won't be safe from Kat's planning."

"I don't know about any planning," Mateo declared. "I was just supposed to check on the dog, and, when I went to the house, it was clear the missing family had left in a hurry. Next thing I knew, Maraya had come running because she thought maybe I was the missing family. They'd been gone for ten days, and she couldn't get any traction when she raised the alarm with the local authority."

"That's just weird," Jacks stated.

"But that's the thing, nobody else cares." Mateo quickly told them about the sheriff taking credit for Timmy's rescue and about the innuendo he had planted at the hospital. Then he filled them in on what Badger had done with the news article. They laughed as soon as he pulled it up and passed his phone between them.

"Good God," Jacob muttered, staring at him. "You know you're a small-time hick when you get to hijack things like that."

"Yeah, but this is a guy who got his ex-wife sectioned." Then he explained what happened and what Badger had found.

They stared at him. "And Badger says she's clear?" Jacks asked.

"Not only clear but the doctor didn't find any reason for concern about suicide or mental health in general. He was quite confused as to why she'd been brought in."

"Yeah, well, we know why," Jacks snapped. "Jesus, that takes the cake."

"And yet we've seen it before where people in law enforcement take advantage," Jacob noted, shaking his head. "They get a taste of authority, then get a little too big for their britches and start making other people pay."

"I know," Mateo muttered. "I was just hoping she wasn't

dealing with that much of an asshole, but finding out that she had been put up for study and investigation because of supposedly wanting to commit suicide takes the cake, especially considering all she's been through. As she told me, if she would ever do that, she would have done it way earlier," and, with that, he explained what else had happened to her.

Both men were in shock. "Jesus, she's been through the wringer."

"I know, and I feel as if it's not quite over yet. She's never quite free of the effects because of Riley."

"She'll have to leave here to be rid of him."

"She's been here all her life."

Jacks added, "Yeah, but it hasn't been a great life."

Jacob nodded in agreement.

Mateo sighed. "I already told her that maybe it's time to get rid of this place. Yet she's always lived here, and this is her family home that her parents left to her."

Jacks looked at him with a sly grin. "You could always convince her to come back and help you out, or you can bring her home to our place."

"Sure," he replied skeptically, "but she's also got a job, and she owns the house. I'm not sure she'll want to go so far away from home."

"This isn't home for her," Jacob clarified immediately. "No way this is home. It may be what she knows, but it's been more like purgatory for her."

Mateo grimaced. "I don't know how many years it's been—three, four, five, ten, whatever it is—but she's had no peace, no joy in her world for a very long time. The best thing she can do is get the hell out and start fresh somewhere."

Jacks immediately agreed.

"And that's all fine and dandy," Mateo added, "but, first off, we need to find out what happened to this little boy and find the rest of his family." Then he told them what his theory was.

They looked at him and frowned. "Holy shit, man, that takes a lot of gall."

"Not if we were being watched and they wanted us to find the boy and to get him some help. Which would imply that the family is held captive, as the father's basically still fighting a war in his head. Yet he is clear-headed enough about what's happening to still get help for his boy. That's just a theory," he clarified. "I don't have anything else to offer right now."

"No, but it's not a bad one. We've seen guys come back from deployment in pretty rough shape, their headspace just not there for families and kids," Jacks acknowledged, "always looking over their shoulder and sometimes completely unaware of their actual surroundings anymore."

"And that's what I'm leaning toward, but again we can't jump to any conclusions." And they went silent as they quickly got out, and headed toward the woods.

"One thing we need to consider, since three of us are here, assuming we have somebody like that out there," Jacks suggested, "is how well-armed is this Carlos guy? And will he take kindly to us snooping around, looking for the rest of his family?"

Mateo shook his head and added, "I sure wouldn't, if it was me. How about you?"

Jacks frowned and nodded. "Which means that, from the minute we head out, we're basically facing somebody who doesn't want us around and is likely to see us as a threat."

"I know." Jacob shared a glance with Jacks, then looked over at Mateo.

"Now that we all know what the stakes are, let's go. The sooner we find this guy, the better."

CHAPTER 7

MARAYA PUTTERED AROUND, then sent several texts to Mateo, asking how close they were and if they'd seen any sign of anything, yet getting very short answers. She frowned at that because, in her heart of hearts, what she was really hoping for was a quick in and out, yet nothing so far. She got to work cleaning up the house, and, by the time she came downstairs, having changed out the bedding and swept the floors upstairs, she brushed the hair off her face and heard a car door slam. She raced to the front door and opened it, then frowned. It was Riley.

He glared at her. "What the hell were you thinking?" he asked.

"I don't know what you're talking about," she snapped. "I didn't talk to anybody. Who the hell are you to accuse me of that shit?"

He stopped in his tracks and looked at her. "What are you, stupid? Or do you think we are?"

She shouldn't be surprised that he wasn't making sense. "You thought that nobody else would know? Really?"

He just snorted.

"Will you just say whatever you came to say and get the hell off my porch?"

"So, you have a new lover, I understand. That'll go over well in town. Say goodbye to ever teaching again."

She should have known that's what this was all about. She shook her head. "Seriously? You're still trying to ruin my career?"

"You shouldn't have a career anyway," he barked, with a wave of his hands.

"That's just bullshit." She stared at him. "I hear you're dating, so what's wrong with my dating?" Not that one should have anything to do with the other, but something about his attitude made her want to piss him off.

He glared at her. "My life has nothing to do with you."

"Oh, oh, right. I'm superglad to hear that," she declared, "because believe me that I don't want anything to do with your life and haven't for a very long time." That didn't go over well either.

"Who the hell is this stranger anyway?" Riley asked, stomping up the front steps.

She immediately closed the door behind her to keep him out and replied, "None of your fucking business." She could see his rage building and realized she wasn't being the most diplomatic, considering she was alone. If Mateo was here, it would be a different story. In fact he would probably welcome it, but she did not and would never welcome any response from this guy. He was already on her shit list for having terrified her before.

"Pretty mouthy, considering who you're talking to," he muttered in that very slow conversational tone that always seemed to accompany his mean streak.

"Not really," she argued, crossing her arms over her chest. She glanced down at her watch and realized that wouldn't tell her anything. She'd been waiting for what seemed like forever for the men to get back, but to have no information for so long made it seem unlikely that they would show up in time to help her right now. Not as if anybody had ever been there to rescue her. "And what do you want anyway?"

"Well now, since you didn't come in to give your statement," he began, with a snide look in her direction, "I just figured maybe you were full of shit and didn't have a statement to give."

She stared at him. "Is that what this is all about?" She snorted. "I can't imagine that'll go over well with Mateo."

"Mateo," he repeated in a mocking tone. "Jesus Christ, what the hell has this random stranger got to do with anything?"

"Considering that he's here for the War Dog that Carlos had, I imagine quite a bit."

"What do you mean, War Dog?"

She sighed, wishing Thorny was with her now. And Mateo. That would change Riley's tune. "You know perfectly well that the dog Carlos had was a K9 War Dog that was shipped overseas and served his time, just like Carlos did."

"I don't give a shit about who served their time. I don't give a crap about any of it, beyond what matters here in my town," he bellowed, red in the face. "What the hell has this got to do with what's going on here now?"

"I don't know," she said, glaring back at him. "I'm the one who asked you guys to look for the missing family, remember?"

"There wasn't anything to find, *remember?* We did go look."

"Bullshit," she snapped, calling him out on that one. "Nobody went looking, and you know it. Nobody gave a shit at all, and here we are."

He stared at her. "You're getting mighty cocky, and

you've got no reason to treat me like that," he snapped.

"Really?" she replied, wondering where her bravado was coming from, knowing that she really should just shut up, but it was hard when it had been a very long time getting to this point. "I don't know what's going on in *your* world," she stated, "but Mateo and I found the little boy from the same family who went missing, the one you didn't care about."

"I told you that we looked," he spat. "Nobody was in the house, nothing in terms of their bank accounts were being used, nothing. So don't you go accusing me of not doing my job," he stated, glaring at her. "You ain't got no call for that."

"*Right.*" She huffed, staring at him. "Maybe you were doing something else in your spare time, but not a one of you came out here and searched the woods."

"Why the hell would I come out and search the woods? No idiot would go out there to begin with and sure as hell wouldn't take his family."

"But you don't know that, and considering that we just found Timmy out there, maybe that's exactly where they went."

He turned and stared off in the distance. "I suppose it's a possibility," he muttered reluctantly. "What the hell are you doing getting mixed up in this shit anyway?"

She shook her head. "Good God, Riley, I'm not *mixed up in* anything. I am just trying to find the family."

"So, you go stomping through the woods, and, sure enough, just like that, you find the boy?"

"Oh, thank you for at least admitting that we were the ones who found the boy."

He flushed at that. "I had to ask my deputies about it this morning, after I saw the article. They told me that you found him, you and some guy. I came straight over to figure out who he was. We don't like strangers in town."

She rolled her eyes. "That's part of the problem. Nobody here likes anybody."

"Strangers are strangers," he declared. "I'm not a big fan of them."

"It doesn't matter if you're a fan of theirs or not," she retorted sharply. "Besides, you're supposed to be nice to people."

"We are nice to people," he countered, "but that doesn't mean everybody wants strangers here."

"You've also got a team full of racists."

"Hey, look. I know Rodney's got strong opinions about any of the immigrants we have in the country," Riley conceded, "but he doesn't speak for all of us." She shook her head at him, and he shifted his hat off his head, held it in his hands, and added, "So don't go judging all of us so quickly."

She stared at him, aware that he was tamer than usual. "Wow, your new ladylove must be having a good effect on you." He glared at her, and she shrugged. "Because you made a statement that almost sounded as if you were a decent human being, but I'm not so sure if it's strong enough to take hold or not."

He glared at her. "And that's enough out of you."

"Sure, it is, of course," she muttered, with a snort. "Interesting tactic."

The sheriff held up a hand. "All I'm saying is Rodney shouldn't have said what he said. I get that he's pretty riled up. I mean, his girl did take off with somebody, as you and the rest of the town know."

"Sure," she agreed, "but that doesn't mean he has the right to hate all Mexicans, all blacks, all of any other nationality in this world just because his girlfriend left him for somebody else. Maybe he should look at his own behavior and think about why she left him."

He glared at her. "I didn't come here to talk relationships."

"I'm really glad to hear that," she muttered, "because that's the last thing I want to talk about with you."

He stormed back to his truck and then stopped, turned to her, and added, "It really wasn't that bad, you know? You didn't have to leave."

She stared at him, her jaw literally dropping. "No. It was ten times worse than *bad*," she retorted, her tone hard, with no give in it. "You came this close," she replied, as she pinched her fingers together, "to bashing my head in. Believe me that's not a situation I would stay in."

He flushed, looked around at the area, and muttered, "I wouldn't have actually hit you."

"Yeah, you would have, and you would have taken me out and deep-sixed me somewhere where nobody would have found me," she added. "And you made sure I knew it. I haven't forgotten any of that, Riley."

He kicked the door shut to his truck and stormed back her way. "You've got no call to say that to me," he roared.

"Yeah, and why is that?" She crossed her arms over her chest, again wondering why the hell she hadn't just kept her mouth shut. "Are you afraid your new lover won't want anything to do with you?"

He glared at her. "I don't know whether I want anything to do with her or not," he declared, "but you ain't messing up my chances."

"Oh, you mean like what you did with my job? Like you did when you got me sectioned for supposedly wanting to kill myself?" She glared at him. "Oh, don't you worry. I've got lots to tell her and the rest of the world. Maybe I should write a memoir. What do you think?"

The color drained from his face, and he turned pale. Then he took several steps forward and whispered, "No way in hell I'll let you ruin my career. I've worked damn hard to get here, and I'm not letting a whore like you ruin my reputation."

"A whore like me?" she repeated softly, wondering how she could ever have thought Riley would be a safe place to land when her whole world had imploded around her. "Wow. Now that would be something for the book for sure. Nothing quite like calling out your ex, whom you absolutely despised and had sectioned for absolutely no reason, then calling her a whore. I'm still talking to my lawyers about that."

Again his face paled. "Look. I thought you were that dangerous."

"You thought no such thing," she spat, "and no way in hell anybody will believe that shit now because you already made them look ridiculous, and they'll remember. I'm not alone anymore," she added, "and I do have friends. I have people helping to ensure I don't get bullied and pushed around. So, you can just take all those threats and that shitty behavior you've hassled me with for all these years and get out of here, or I swear there will be a price to pay."

He stepped forward quickly, his fists coming out, and she felt her legs quaking, realizing that this could be the one time he did kill her. "Remember that part about you saying you would never ever hit me? That was a damn lie. You knocked me unconscious how many times?"

"Not enough," he muttered, through his teeth, "but

that's all right because you've got one more coming." With that, he grabbed her by her shoulder and jerked her around hard.

THE TRUCK CAME to a hard stop, and Mateo got out and raced toward the front steps with the other two men right behind him. Thorny beat him to the porch and to Maraya, where he growled and barked at Riley.

"I don't think so, asshole. Let her go, or you'll be dead before you hit the ground." As soon as the man who was threatening Maraya turned and glared at him, Mateo saw the sheriff's star and the name on his shirt. Mateo got right in his face. "Is this how you keep order around here? Police brutality?" he asked. "You come over here to hassle a woman alone at her place?"

"Who the fuck are you?" he roared.

Shoving his face even closer to the sheriff's, Mateo stated, "Somebody you sure as hell better get to know, just in case you don't already. Things have changed around here, and you don't get to push people around. You don't get to spread lies about people, and you don't get to claim rescues that had nothing to do with you or your shitty officers, who declined to get out to do another search last night when there could well have been a trail to follow," he snapped at him.

"This isn't Lone Ranger shit, and the position of sheriff isn't there so you can take advantage of the citizens in this town," Mateo snapped. "I gather you're the piece-of-shit sheriff. Hard to miss since you sure keep advertising it constantly."

The sheriff's face had turned a blustery red, then different shades of white and green as he seemed about to blow a gasket. However, when he saw two other men in front of him, all with the same hard look as Mateo's, Riley paused.

Mateo nodded. "Yeah, take a good look. We're not the kind of people who yell and harass and threaten women with physical violence," he shared in a low and deadly tone. "And you can sure as hell bet that your constituents will find out about this."

At that, Riley laughed. "It won't matter one damn bit. As far as they're all concerned, I should have beaten the crap out of her when I was married to her. Or did you not know that part, lover boy?" he asked, a hard look sent his way. "You don't know anything about me or what this bitch has put me through."

"I really don't care because nothing she could have done deserves that fist you were ready to slam in her face."

At that, the sheriff looked down at his clenched fists and immediately tried to open them, but his fists remained clenched, along with his temper.

Thorny growled again, earning a hard look from Riley, who put his hand on his gun only to have Mateo say, "Oh hell no. It's time for you to let go," Mateo snapped. "Time for you to let her move on, and you just go be you—whatever that is—but away from her. Obviously the relationship between the two of you was toxic as hell, but you don't have to keep it that way, and you don't have to keep threatening her with whatever it is you think she's done." He looked over at Maraya. "Are you okay?"

She nodded. He immediately opened up one arm, and she stepped up closer to him. He pulled her tightly against him and stated, "He won't hurt you."

"Not this time," she declared, glaring at the sheriff.

He studied her, then turned to the sheriff. Still facing him, Mateo asked her, "Has he ever raised a hand to you before?"

She nodded. "Yes, he called it discipline," she said in a low voice.

Mateo swore at that. "Is that the kind of man you are?" he asked, with a hard look in Riley's direction again. "A man who can't control his temper and who can't make a woman love him? Is beating the crap out of women the only way you can get them to be nice to you?"

The sheriff's face turned muddy colors, and Jacks stepped up behind him and placed a hand on his shoulder. "And just in case you think these two are alone, they're not," he added, spoken in a hard tone himself. "We're all military. We've all seen this shit before, and not one of us will stand for it."

Without a word, the sheriff turned and headed down the steps and back to his truck.

"Nice to meet you," Mateo called out in a sarcastic tone. "Stop by again soon." The sheriff got into his vehicle and slammed the door so hard that Mateo was afraid the window would drop inside the door, as it rattled so badly. Thorny delivered a final bark of warning as he drove off.

As soon as the vehicle turned around and left, Mateo looked down at Maraya, still standing in the circle of his arms. "He didn't get a shot in, did he?"

She shook her head. "No, not this time." She scrubbed at her face. "God, I thought I was past that fear, that sense of being frozen. Yet, as soon as he raises a fist, I feel as if I haven't grown at all."

"You've grown just fine," Jacob stated in a comforting

voice. "You didn't cower, and you didn't run. Men like that, they want to see fear. They want you to run. They want you to be terrified. It's the only way they can feel empowered."

She turned to Mateo. "Riley definitely won't forgive you for what you said."

"I don't give a crap if he does or not," Mateo replied, with a smile. "Now how about some coffee?"

She looked at him, blinked several times, and then gave her head a shake. "Oh, God, the search. How did you guys do?" She turned, looking from one to the other. "Did you find anyone?" The men looked at her, shared a glance with Mateo, and their expressions revealed more than they did.

Mateo added, "Come on. Let's go get coffee."

She stared at him and whispered, "And all that means no then."

"It means no, but it's not a blanket no," he clarified. "We did need to come back in, but we'll go back out again."

She searched his gaze intently. "That would imply something was there."

He turned her around, gently pushed her back into the house, Thorny jumped in front of him to stay close to her. Once inside Mateo replied, "Come on. Let me put on some coffee, and get you away from that lovely vision of the sheriff out there."

"He's an asshole," she stated succinctly.

He chuckled. "He absolutely is, and he's apparently also a wife-beater. You left out that part earlier."

"He would call it discipline," she repeated.

His jaw worked at that, and he nodded. "Yeah, I've heard a couple men refer to their asshole actions as discipline or teaching family members a lesson, but that's not the way. These guys are weak. They're cowards, and they can only feel big and strong by hurting others who are much more vulnerable," he stated, as he walked with the other men through to the kitchen. There, he efficiently put on coffee, having sorted out the coffeemaker earlier that morning. He turned to look at her, still standing in the middle of the room, looking lost. "Ah, sweetheart, it'll be fine."

She looked up at him and whispered, "I don't even know why I'm still here." Then she turned and looked around at the house.

"Because it's what you know," he stated, "and what we know tends to dominate what we do. The devil you know and all that."

"Maybe, but Riley's a hell of a devil, and I don't want to know him any more than I already do."

"Good, then you need to start making plans."

"But this is my house," she pointed out. "This is all I have."

"It's a good house. It's also your family home, but I'm not sure that you need to stay here for any particular reason. You could get a job teaching anywhere in the country."

"Until they do a background search on me and find out I was institutionalized."

Mateo nodded. "Badger is looking into that. Maybe there's a way to wipe the record clean."

She nodded. "That might help." She sighed. "I know it sounds bad that I've stayed all this time, and I had been thinking about it again for a while. Yet, once the family next door went missing, I found it impossible to even think about walking away. I know at some point there will be nothing I can do, but, up until now, I hadn't really felt as if I'd hit that point. I wanted to stay as long as I could do something, so I did. I didn't want to just leave and have them be forgotten."

CHAPTER 8

MARAYA SAT IN the kitchen, Thorny stretched out nearby on the wood floor, her mind going back over the events of the last thirty minutes, and she looked over at Mateo and said, "I think I'm ready to move."

His eyebrows shot up, and he studied her closely. "I'm not against it," he shared. "I just need to confirm that you won't make a snap decision that you'll regret later on."

She glared at him. "Five minutes ago, you were telling me to sort myself out and to look at other options."

"And I'm glad that you are looking at other options," he agreed, with a nod. He sat down, then motioned for the two other men to join them, making for a warm, cozy group.

Maraya realized that one of the things she was missing in her life was friends. Here she had been alone with some guy she'd met just a little over a day before, and now he had friends for her as well. Yet, for the last several years, she had been more or less ostracized because of her divorce, and it had been a difficult place to find herself.

She'd filled her life with everything else and hadn't deliberately pushed people away. However, people were pushing her away, so it just became easier for her to push away first. People in town were cordial enough, but it was all quite superficial.

"Just seeing the three of you here, I don't even know

whether or not you know each other." All three nodded. "See? That is something I don't have here. I literally have no friends. Plenty of acquaintances but no real friends. I can't really have friends here because of who my ex is. I've lost every single person in my life who's important to me, and yet I'm still clinging to this bit of wood." She sighed, as she looked around her ancestral home. "I'm not even sure why anymore."

"Because it's what you do know," Mateo offered, "because it's familiar, because it's a connection to your parents, and it's comforting, which is what you need when the rest of your life is stressed to the max."

"I didn't think I was stressed that badly," she replied, "until I saw Riley here at my house and of course what came out of his mouth—" She shuddered.

"Did you never call the police?" Jacks asked. She gave him a wry look, and then he winced. "Okay, stupid question. He is the police—sheriff, in this case."

"Exactly, although he wasn't always the sheriff," she clarified. "The divorce lawyer I hired wasn't from town, and he helped me get through the whole process, but it wasn't easy. Without his help, I don't think I would have gotten that done either."

"Probably not," Mateo said, just as the coffee finished dripping.

She watched him get up, completely comfortable in her kitchen, as he walked over, poured cups for all of them, and brought them back. Thorny kept his eyes on his movements but didn't leave from her side. "That's amazing," she murmured, staring at Mateo.

"What?" he asked, giving her a quizzical glance.

"Just the confidence to get up, to make coffee, and to

serve it," she explained. "Riley would never have done that in one million years."

"It doesn't take confidence," Mateo added. "It just takes the willingness to get up off your butt and do it."

She laughed. "You can bet that isn't something Riley is prepared to do, not if he has anybody around who will do it for him."

"So, he's not only a jerk but a lazy ass to boot," he noted, with a casual shrug. "He's not your concern anymore."

"He is if he comes back after you're gone," she pointed out. His gaze turned her way, and she felt almost pinned in place.

"Is that a possibility? I thought I heard he was dating somebody in town."

"Of course it is a possibility," she declared.

"I get the impression he's still hooked on you," Jacob stated stiffly.

"And I don't know why," she replied. "It was not a good time between us."

"Maybe not, but, if he thinks you're the one who got away, anything else might not matter to a guy like him."

"I'm not even sure that I got away as much as I fell into a trap," she clarified. "When I first left him, it did occur to me that maybe his brother didn't die of natural causes, but that's just foolish."

The men looked at each other, and Mateo asked, his tone careful, "Why would that be foolish? I mean, he died at the same time as your parents, right?"

"He was in the same accident." The men exchanged glances, and that made her uncomfortable as hell. "And, yes, he died."

"It doesn't matter anymore," Jacks suggested. "If you're

serious about relocating, you need to look at things like selling the house and figuring out where you want to go instead."

"Sure, and that's easier said than done. No matter where I go, I'll have to find a job."

Jacks continued. "Property prices in this area are probably pretty solid, and you've got a great place here." He faced her and added, "You may very well do okay out of this."

"Depends where I end up," she replied, with a wry look in his direction. "Property prices in other parts of the country are deadly."

He nodded. "They absolutely are, but you're not compelled to go to one of those."

"No, but I would like to go someplace where there is more money for teaching, where people put more credence into education, and where a woman has at least some value," she clarified. "I've pretty well had enough of being a doormat."

"Good," Mateo agreed, with a bright smile. "And, by the way, I haven't seen much of a doormat since I've been here."

She burst out laughing. "Yeah, you caught me on a good day." The men grinned at each other. She just smiled and admitted, "Mateo has been good for me. … I was so worried and so stressed about everything going on in my world that losing the neighbor family at the same time was just too much. I think, in a way, I was losing myself."

"That's deep," Jacks said, with a nod, "and yet it makes sense. It's really important for you to do what you need to do for yourself. If moving is what will get you out of this hellish situation"—he looked around—"personally I would be all over it. But sometimes we cling to what we know because change is scary."

"Change *is* scary," she acknowledged, with a nod. "On the other hand, the thought of Riley continuing to smear my name in town, coming to my door, always with those same threats, no thank you," she declared. "Some things have to be worth changing for."

"And you are worth getting through a change, even a big one," Mateo pointed out. "You need to do things for you."

"Sure." She gave him half a smile, then lifted her coffee cup. "Now, enough about my mess, enough about me. Fill me in."

"We found tracks out there of different people," Mateo began, "and I think we were right to consider that Carlos has a bunker or something out there."

"So then why put Timmy out in the woods like that?" she asked, her eyes widening in horror.

"Because I think he saw us. I think he realized we were probably a good way for Timmy to get some help. So Carlos put Timmy out there with Thorny, just like we were thinking."

"He was still taking an awful chance."

"He did, and you know any court of law would probably take the child away from him because of that."

"I know," she muttered. "What about the other family members?"

"We didn't see anybody, but we'll head out this afternoon for another look," he shared. "Do you have anybody here you can stay with?"

Surprised, she frowned at him as she slowly lowered her coffee cup. "Why?"

He hesitated, looked back at Jacks and Jacob, and shrugged. "We don't want your lovely sheriff to return in the meantime."

"I don't think he will now." She studied his face carefully. "Yet you are right in that I can't be sure. He doesn't like being thwarted, and he thinks he's the big cheese around here. I'm sure, in his mind, you failed to give him the respect he was due," she noted, with a hint of humor.

"I'm sure I didn't," Mateo agreed, with a gleeful smile. "Guys like that never seem to think that they get what they deserve and always think the world owes them."

"I would volunteer to give him what he deserves," Jacks quipped, and they all shared a laugh.

Maraya sighed. "That's the way he's been his whole life. The world owes him. His brother owed him. No matter what, Riley's always had a chip on his shoulder. Still, I don't think he would have had anything to do with his brother's death."

"You started to tell us about that earlier, so what was going on?"

"My parents and my fiancé were all in the same accident," she began, "but my mother and father died instantly. Joseph hung on to life. The docs thought he would survive, but then he didn't. There was some air embolism or something. I don't know. They thought he was fine, and then suddenly he wasn't, and it was a shock to everyone. After the car accident, losing both my parents, and the roller coaster ride with my fiancé, honest to God, I was just numb. It was one more bad news scenario added to the others."

"Of course," Mateo replied, as he glanced at the other men, just to see them exchanging glances.

She added, "You guys really don't know Riley like I do."

"And that brings us back to the matter at hand. Will you be okay here alone?"

"Of course," she stated, "and, if I'm not, I've got bigger

problems because he'll still be here after you guys are gone."

"I know," Mateo muttered. "I just wasn't sure if you had considered that aspect or not. If you don't mind, we'll grab some food, possibly some medical supplies, and head back—" Interrupted by a *woof,* he looked down to see Thorny at his side, staring at him.

"What do you want, boy?" he asked. Another *woof* came, and Mateo looked over at his buddies. They both immediately got up and headed to the windows.

"So, are you seriously thinking the dog is warning us about something?" she asked, studying the men curiously. "You went for the windows as if Thorny was telling you something."

"We did because we've worked with these War Dogs before, and their instincts are amazing," Jacks shared warmly. "It's just calming for us to actually pay attention."

"I'm glad you do," she said, looking down at Thorny. "Take him back out with you." When Mateo hesitated, she frowned at him. "What?"

"I was thinking about leaving him here with you, just in case Riley comes back."

"I don't think he will," she repeated.

"But it would be better if we did find the family and didn't have to worry about you so much," Jacob added, with a smile.

Mateo gave her a lopsided look. "I'm all for finding out what's going on with the family," he clarified, "but they have been gone for quite a while. Right now, I'm more concerned about making sure *you* don't go missing."

"You really think Riley will come back, don't you?" she asked.

"Guys like that don't like being thwarted," he pointed

out. "As I consider his behavior, I think just enough anger was there to cause quite a bit more trouble."

"Sure," she muttered. "Riley's just *that guy.*"

"I understand," Mateo acknowledged, "and that's why I'm concerned."

"Go find Carlos and the rest of his family. That's first and foremost," she declared. "I'll hole up here, and I'll be fine. Take Thorny with you. If I see Riley coming back, I'll leave the house and head into the backwoods."

"As long as you stay in touch," Mateo stated. "We can't have you disappearing. I don't want to find myself looking for you too."

"That's a novel thought," she quipped, with a smile. "I don't think I've ever had anybody prepared to even go looking."

"Times have changed," Mateo stated pointedly. "Now"—he hopped up, staring at her—"do you mind if I rustle up some sandwiches?"

"God no. And I feel terrible because I'll let you."

He burst out laughing. "We know how to rustle up our own grub," he added, still chuckling. "So that's really not an issue. Just sit and relax. We've got this."

And she watched in amazement, as the men worked together and very quickly had a stack of sandwiches wrapped up to take with them. Mateo walked over with a sandwich on a plate and said, "This is for you." She smiled at him. "I don't know when we'll be back, so you eat while we're gone."

She cracked a smile. "Yes, *Dad.*"

He rolled his eyes. "I hardly see myself in that role," he muttered.

Her eyes widened as she heard the note in his tone. "Not

exactly meaning it that way either," she replied. "On the other hand, you've done a hell of a job taking care of me when I seemingly wasn't quite ready or capable of doing it myself," she admitted. "If nothing else, I appreciate your defending me with Riley."

He smiled. "Shouldn't have to defend yourself with that asshole," he grumbled, "but we'll deal with that after we've dealt with this." He looked over at the others. "Ready?" As one, they all got up and headed to the door.

She felt that sense of loss already. "Please be careful."

"We will," Jacob replied. "And the same to you. If Riley comes back, you don't have to talk to him."

"I know, and, if he comes back, I'll leave."

"Good," he noted. "And if those deputies of his—the ones we saw yesterday—if they come back, you be long gone."

"Yeah, I think in a way they're a whole lot worse than their boss," she shared, "but I can't be sure of that."

"Keep away from all of them," Mateo added. Then he walked over and gave her a gentle hug. "We will be back tonight. I'm just not sure when."

"That's good news," Maraya said. "I presume you're staying here then."

He winced. "I assumed that the offer still stood, but you're right. That was taking on a lot."

She laughed. "No, it's not," she countered, as she looked at the other two. "You guys are welcome to stay here too."

The men nodded politely. "Thanks, but we already grabbed a motel room in town, but we'll drop him off." And, with that, they were gone.

MATEO WATCHED AS she stood on the front step and waved at them.

"For somebody who wouldn't get involved, you seem to be involved," Jacks pointed out.

"Wasn't thinking I was getting involved at all," Mateo explained. "Nothing quite like seeing a man, particularly somebody in law enforcement, ready to drive his fist into a woman's jaw to make you realize that you need to take another look at things."

"Another look at what though?" Jacks asked, facing him. "At her, at the situation, or at your single status?"

"All of it, I guess. I'm not sure how it works," Mateo admitted, "but, yeah, definitely something is there."

"Oh, we could see that," Jacob declared, with a smile. "Besides, we're pretty accustomed to Kat lighting a spark, then watching from the sidelines."

"That woman has some innate ability." Jacks laughed, saying that.

"I don't know about that," Mateo added. "I've never really seen it in action before, but, if you're putting this down to Kat's abilities, then maybe."

They drove down the road to the point where they had come out last time, having mapped a bit of the entrance and exit. As per their previous plan, they split up. Mateo had Thorny with him. He wanted to leave him with Maraya, but Thorny had made it very clear that he was coming. As Mateo hopped out, Thorny came too and stuck by his side.

Jacks noted, "Interesting that the dog has chosen you."

"I'm not sure why, but I'm guessing it's because I found the little boy," Mateo suggested. "We do know what loyalty is like with these animals."

"Absolutely, and we're grateful that this guy is happy to

be around, but he might not be able to stay with the family, if any family is even left. He certainly won't be able to stay with the little boy."

"I know," Mateo muttered. "I don't know whether the dog would be happy to transfer his affection in my direction or not. It could be hard on him too."

"It definitely would be hard on him, but that doesn't mean it's not something he'll do." And, with that, the three men, having synced their watches, quietly headed out into the night.

Mateo ran on the assumption that Carlos had taken his family underground somewhere, and just enough miles of tree cover and brush were out here for Carlos to build some decent camouflage. He would avoid building fires, as that would give away his position. Luckily the nighttime weather wasn't cold enough that he would need one to keep them warm, but it would be hard to live on cold food the entire time out here.

Mateo headed to the northeast corner of the grid that they had mapped off, with Thorny staying easily at his side. As soon as he reached the designated spot, he sent out an owl's hoot and listened for a response from the other men. Almost instantly he got both responses. That was the thing about working with pros. Everybody knew what to do, and they operated seamlessly, without any issues.

Mateo hunkered down in his spot and waited. Sure enough, he lifted his nose to the smell of a campfire. He smiled and sent out a single hoot and got a single one back. They'd likely gotten a whiff of the same thing, and that was the most encouraging thing Mateo had heard so far. He casually headed toward the smell, the location of the campfire, knowing that it would be important to move in quietly.

Carlos was probably fully armed and prepared to keep his family safe by whatever means possible, and it's likely that living in the forest was what he currently considered to be the best thing for his own safety and that of his family. Unfortunately, if he was dealing with PTSD, he could consider everyone as the enemy, and Carlos would be the first to shoot, on the grounds that it was self-defense, sincerely believing that to be true.

The last thing Mateo wanted to do was end up causing a scene that would have all of them go down in an exchange of gunfire. Even if they all died out here, Mateo didn't know whether the sheriff would finally do something about the hunt for the rest of the family or not. Since Mateo and Jacks and Jacob had been out here on their own, Mateo figured Riley helping would be unlikely. Mateo crept forward, Thorny at his side, moving softly in the night.

It could be just them out here, which Mateo wasn't against either. It was a beautiful evening, and to even think that this gorgeous country, where peace and quiet were offered, could be turned into violence, fear, and pain was just sad—especially if a war veteran had likely disassociated from his present reality and had been caught up by the demons of his past. Mateo sighed, shaking his head, staring out again at the stunningly beautiful night.

For whatever reason, that brought Maraya back to his mind. He hoped she was following his instructions and staying hunkered down. The last thing he wanted was something to happen to her while he was out here.

The sheriff had pissed him off just enough that Mateo was also very wary of anything that the man promised, and leaving her alone was not something Mateo wanted to do.

Riley really had a hate on for her, and it was disheartening to see. It was so typical that women all over the world were taken advantage of in one way or another, in situations where they had almost no ability to fight back. Her ex had more or less taken her career from her and had completely demolished her reputation within the town. Sadly Mateo wasn't sure anybody here even cared.

She had no support system, no family, and, from what he could tell, no friends either, and that just made her life here incredibly hard and singularly lonely. Not an existence he would wish for anybody.

An owl hooted off to the left, immediately pulling Mateo's attention back to the job at hand. He changed course ever-so-slightly and, with Thorny at his side, he pressed forward.

CHAPTER 9

M ARAYA SIGHED. BEING left behind wouldn't have been too bad if Mateo hadn't mentioned the possibility that her beloved ex-husband might come back on his own. She would have been fine, but—Mateo having planted that seed, probably thinking of her own protection and being sensible—still, it was hard to get that thought out of her mind. And that was depressing because, if there was one thing she hated, it was confrontation. She'd handled herself with Riley this time, but, if Mateo and friends hadn't showed up when they did, she may well have been punched in the face—or worse.

She paced the house, ate the sandwich Mateo had made for her, and thought about making dinner, a proper meal this time, and very quickly ran through everything else she could think of to do. Still, there was no sign of Mateo and his friends and no other visitors. The visitor part she was grateful for, but the rest of it? Not so much. And the more she thought about it, the more determined she was to sell the house and leave this place.

She didn't have a destination in mind, but almost anywhere would be better than here at this point. She just needed to make more of a solid plan first. If she could sell and get out with limited effort, she would be grateful. One of her older friends with whom she had gone to school was in real estate, but she was also fairly hooked up to the network of local churches. So the odds of Maraya getting an unbiased opinion regarding the potential for sale seemed limited. If anything, it might lead straight to Riley, and the last thing she wanted was for him to know she was looking to sell.

She didn't think he would let her go easily, and yet why not? It's not as if they had a healthy relationship, and, if she were honest, they never had. A lot of that was her fault. She'd gotten sucked into a plan by somebody who, in all reality, had taken advantage of her grief. Riley brought Maraya into his life and into a position she never would have entered if it hadn't been for the loss of everybody in her world. But she had gotten herself into the situation, so it was up to her to get out of it.

She frowned as she continued to pace around the house, wondering just what this property would be worth and what that would look like for her if she lived elsewhere. She had no idea where to go, but warmer sounded good. She wasn't against a little bit of winter, but she'd been living in this area for a long time. She wasn't too interested in going into heavy, ugly winters. She also didn't want to go where it was terribly populated.

She decided to go for a walk just to get her head together, something that she'd always been comfortable doing as a way to maintain her own sanity. It used to drive her ex crazy, but, for her, it was a way of finding peace in a world gone crazy, finding some solace in the silence, when otherwise none was to be found. As she walked around the property with a new perspective, assessing it, looking at how much land it was, wondering just what kind of value she would be looking at, she suddenly heard an odd sound.

She froze and turned to her left, but nothing was there, at least nothing she could see. Not sure what she heard, she moved quickly back toward the house, thinking that's where safety lay, not even sure what she was afraid of. However, as she got within sight of the house, she immediately stepped back behind the trees. In front of her were the deputies. Of all the things that she had considered, this was not one of them.

She immediately pulled out her phone and started videotaping them. They walked around, calling out for her, and, when there was no sign of her, they started laughing and calling her names, as if that gave them a release of some kind from their frustration. Obviously they'd taken a bit of ribbing because of the article that had been published on the internet about who had rescued whom, but she didn't understand why they were back again. It sure as hell wasn't anything good.

Mateo had definitely called it. She was too far away to hear what they were saying, but it sounded as if pretty ribald jokes were told, also not becoming of their positions, but then nothing about them was professional, and it made her all the more worried. When they went back to their truck, she groaned with relief, only to have them pull something out and come back to her house again. It looked very much like—

Was that spray paint?

No way they would spray her house, would they? She kept filming to ensure that, whatever they did, it would go live. Almost instantly they went through one can and then another. She wished she had a way to post it live and then remembered how the community had a communal blog where everybody could post things. She immediately logged into the site and pressed Play, so that her video feed went live at the same time.

The men were laughing and joking and calling her names as they ripped through the spray paint. She knew something horrible was being written all over the front of her house, and that would make it even harder on her. But a can of spray paint was nothing to what she hoped would happen when they found out they were caught in the act. As soon as they were done and got into their vehicle, still howling with laughter, she kept filming their clearly marked vehicle as it left her driveway, then she posted it.

As soon as they were gone, she copied the feed and shared it with every venue she could think of, particularly the sheriffs for the two neighboring jurisdictions. One had often commented on several of the local events, so it was easy to find Riley's account. Almost immediately her video got a series of likes, dislikes, and shares, as people made ribald comments about the deputies' behavior, while others were absolutely furious that somebody would do that.

She stayed hidden, afraid that the deputies would return. More than that, she was afraid to see what they had painted on her house. It was getting colder out here, but she felt safer staying out here in the dark. Especially now that she had taken her stand and had posted that video. She was already afraid that somebody would come back and nail her for it. Surely she had every right to video what people were doing to her property and then share it with the public.

Eventually she did walk around to the front and stared in shock at the words *whore* and *slut* written all across the front of her house. It was sickening to see and was horrible to feel the sense of violation.

When her phone rang, she didn't answer it; she wasn't

even sure who it was. When it rang again, a text came through, stating that he was Mateo's boss, Badger. When she texted back a cautious reply, she immediately got a text back, telling her that he was calling and saying she should answer. Her phone rang again, showing the same number. "Hello?" she answered.

"Did you post those videos?" he asked.

"Yes," she stated defiantly. "What am I supposed to do? Just let those assholes continuously ruin my life?"

"No," he stated, his tone calm. "I'm absolutely thrilled that you did it." She even heard the smile in his tone. "However, now I'm really worried about you, especially if you're alone."

"I'm alone. Mateo and the guys you sent are out looking for the family."

"Good," he noted, "but that means you're alone."

"Yes."

"What do you expect will happen as people see this?"

"Anything and everything. I won't be shocked if I have people coming by just to gawk and to take pictures of my house," she shared. "I suppose I might get some reporters, but they'll be hours away."

"Maybe not," Badger noted. "I don't know if you've realized it yet, but this thing has blown up all over the place. So you'll get more and more phone calls, likely from bigger news outlets as they figure out what's happening," he told her. "Very, very quickly you'll be everywhere. I hate to say it, but your post has gone viral. It's both good and bad, but, right now, I'm mostly concerned about your safety. When these guys realize what you've done, it could get ugly. If you're not out of the house, and you have a place to go, I really want to see you leave."

"I don't have a place to go," she stated, realizing he was serious. "I didn't even think about that when I did this."

"Right, but it needed to happen apparently. You can't have law enforcement running around doing this kind of damage."

"I agree, but the sheriff will let them off with a warning, and the citizens will think it's a big joke."

Silence came on the other end. "Seriously?"

She whispered, "Yes."

"Damn," he muttered. "That means we need to charge everybody involved."

"Yes, and I would like my house back too, so I can sell it," she added, the tears creeping into her eyes, as she realized that she'd just probably ostracized anybody who could make that happen.

"Can you think of anybody who you know who might want to buy it?"

"I doubt it, since it currently says *whore* all over it."

"A can of paint will take care of that," Badger suggested. "That part isn't an issue. Do you know anybody doing any developing in the area or anyone else who could use the land?"

"The neighboring ranch owner maybe. I don't know that it's operating as a ranch, but he's some bigwig and might be interested in expanding his holdings. At one point he was, but I wasn't in any shape to deal with it then. My dear ex," she spat, venom spilling into her tone, "wasn't of the opinion that I should even be allowed to keep the property at the time."

"Good God, he's really a winner, isn't he?"

Maraya snorted.

"Do you know the name of the ranch owner?"

"I think it was Mark Slinger," she muttered. "That could be wrong. I don't know for sure at this moment."

"If I contact him, and he's interested, do you want to sell?"

"Hell yes," she declared. "I need to get out of this town before it kills me."

"That is part of my concern," he agreed.

As he went to hang up, she said, "Wait."

"What is it?" he asked, but no impatience filled his tone. "What can I help you with?"

She asked, "Why are you doing all this?"

He chuckled. When he finally spoke, she heard a gentle smile in his tone. "Because I can. We're not all assholes in this world." And, with that, he ended the call.

MATEO WAS ABOUT to take another step forward when Thorny let out a low growl from deep in his throat. Mateo immediately stepped back and crouched down to see a trap. An old rabbit trap. It would also work great as a warning system. He shook his head and smiled. "At least now I know we're on the right track," he whispered, with a smile. "Who's there?" he asked softly.

No response came.

"Look. I'm not sure how bad your world is right now or how desperate you are to keep this as is, but you do know it's not exactly something we can let slide, not unless your wife and daughter are staying with you in these conditions voluntarily. We need to confirm that they're not being held captive. And what about your son, damn it?" His whispers were loud, even to himself, and he fell silent as he searched his surroundings.

An eeriness filled the air, as if Mateo were being watched. And he could very well be. He needed to be damn sure that he was on the right track, while he looked out for danger at every angle. After all, this Carlos guy was serious and may well feel that the world was out to get him. And, true enough, from Carlos's point of view, it probably looked that way. Sadly, a lot of vets came home in very similar condition and needed months and months of help in order to really feel that the war was over for them.

Mateo wasn't sure that Carlos had ever gotten the help he needed or whether he had just gotten even more paranoid since he'd come home. Right now it didn't matter anymore. Carlos was currently a diehard believer in his version of the world that he was living in, and that would be hard on his family too. Yet Mateo needed to know that the rest of the family was in good shape and was happy to be living out here in the woods. Otherwise no way would Mateo leave them in this situation, stuck with somebody who had a whole different idea of what life would look like in the future.

He took several cautious steps forward, checking intently for traps. Now that he was sure what he was up against, it would be a little bit easier—but not a lot since Carlos was a pro too. He was obviously out to protect himself and his family from a world that was after him.

That was the hard part. He wasn't in the wrong; it's just that it would seem like it to anybody else in the world around him. Unless you were a veteran too, nobody would understand what this guy had been through. Nobody would be there for him. As far as they were concerned, he was the bad guy. And maybe he was, but he hadn't gotten here all on his own.

It was a shitty world for a lot of the vets when they came home, and Mateo had seen them struggle, time and time again. He just didn't want to see anything bad happen to this guy's family because of Carlos's own paranoid fears. And yet it would be hard to take him out of this scenario safely, when everything looked to be harsh for him.

Mateo moved forward a little bit more and noted a trip line up ahead. He saw it just as Thorny growled. He put his hand on the dog's nape and whispered, "It's okay, buddy. I see it." He stepped over the line and had the dog jump over it too. Mateo didn't want to take it down, but he would also keep track of where they were so he could make a quick exit, if need be.

As they continued to move forward, he heard an owl off to the side, much closer than expected. So at least one of his buddies had closed in on them, but they hadn't found what they were looking for either. However, Mateo could sense that feeling of closeness. Carlos and the rest of his family were there, up ahead, and Mateo was almost there too. Yet that *almost* would be the difference between life and death because, if this went wrong, it would go wrong in a bad way.

Thorny nudged him, and he looked down at the dog, staring into the darkness. So Mateo bent down to the dog's eye level to see what he had seen, and, sure enough, a set of eyes stared back at him. He raised his eyebrows ever-so-slightly. "Hello there," he whispered.

The child blinked and stared at him.

"I'm Mateo," he murmured. "Are you all right? Do you need help?"

She looked at him, looked at the dog, and pointed.

"Yes, that's Thorny," Mateo replied, his tone friendly. "We came out here looking for you." All he could think of was that this had to be the missing sister. "We also have Timmy in the hospital, getting help. He's very sick. Are you Donna?"

Her eyes widened, and she stared at him intently.

"Is your daddy out here?"

Immediately fear flared in her gaze, and, although it was dark, it was just light enough to see the shift. She looked directly to the side and then quickly back at Mateo again, unwillingly giving away her father's position.

Mateo smiled and nodded. Instead of moving forward, he stepped back and to the right, just ahead of where she had looked.

As he moved forward, he heard a man growl beside him, "Don't fucking move."

CHAPTER 10

I T WAS ALL Maraya could do to walk into her house, with that nastiness all over the siding in the front. By now, the shock had receded, the anger had fermented and had burned itself out, and all she felt was a deep, abiding sadness. This had been her family home. It had been a place of safety and joy, a place where she had gotten pregnant with the love of her life. It was not a place that she wanted to walk away from with horrible memories, not the way she felt right now. And yet not a whole lot else for her to do here. She had no job she wanted to go to and nobody she wanted to face in town or even to say goodbye to. It was just so damn sad to have her world come crashing down to this end. So unnecessary.

Her phone had been going off steadily, and she checked the number each time. However, unless it was Mateo or his boss, she wasn't answering. When Badger called again, she said, "Hello."

"Are you all right?" he asked.

"Yes, I'm fine."

"You don't sound it."

After a moment of silence, she replied, "It's just sadness at this point. Sadness of what could have been, sadness of what was, and the sadness of more loss." She tried to hold back the tears.

"Of course," Badger agreed. "A lot of the sadness comes

from the death of all hope. When you lose somebody, you also lose the dreams you shared, whether it's a divorce or a death, or somebody just disappears without telling you. It's the cumulative loss of all that, of all you had planned for, had dreamed of, and had hoped for together," he explained.

"Sounds as if you understand."

"I do. In so many ways, I do," he murmured. "Life is what you make it, but sometimes we get thrown these curveballs, and we have to react in a timely manner just to stay afloat. You have an opportunity now to completely shift your life, and that's not a bad thing. I would say it's a good thing, considering what you're experiencing and what to you has become almost normal now," he pointed out. "You do not want to normalize this. You do not want this behavior to be something that you see as being commonplace. It's not. It shouldn't be. Don't make it so."

She sat down with a hard *thump* on the dining room chair. "I'm back inside my house now. I've just been wandering around, thinking about everything that's gone on in the last few years and how different everything could be."

"It could have been if people had lived," he stated brutally. "Sadly, they did not. You might have had a chance to rebuild a life, but you ended up married to someone who clearly doesn't respect women at all. I can't make that any easier on you, but you really do have to pick up and to move forward now."

"And if I don't want to?" she asked, rubbing her eyes, knowing that she sounded like a fool because she really had no other choice here.

"If that's your decision," he noted, "you would have little opportunity for joy in your life. I understand the depression, the sadness. I understand all of it, but you could be much better off, if only you make the move."

"Speaking of which," she asked, "were you able to track down the neighbor?"

"Yes, and that's what I wanted to talk to you about. He would like to buy the property."

She stared down at her phone in astonishment. "Just like that?"

"Yes. Just like that."

"Good God, what are you, a miracle worker?"

"No, but he also heard and saw what happened to your place online today. I don't know if you really understand how viral it has gone. Your neighbor has certainly seen it, as have many of the other locals," he added. "Has anybody come to the house?"

"No, not yet," she muttered. "All the doors are locked, and I'm inside. I'm not answering the phone, and it is ringing off the hook. If it weren't for you or Mateo, I would have gone somewhere else already, anywhere else, but they are coming back here, so I'm here."

"So, in a way, that's another good thing about all this. I told Mateo the latest."

"How did he take it?"

"He was pissed," Badger stated shortly. "So don't you worry about that. We'll still have to determine a sales price, negotiate with your neighbor, but the rancher's very interested in buying you out. He would have suggested it himself after seeing that video because no way he wants you to stay and to deal with these kinds of issues. He mentioned he might even run for sheriff himself next time."

She started to laugh. "Oh my God. That would be hilarious if Riley lost his job, but it would be a hard sell."

"Not really. I guess your neighbor's looking at opening

some business or something locally, and that would be part of his play in order to get support. Besides, he's not a big fan of your sheriff."

"Unless you've lived here all your life, I don't think anybody is," she muttered. "And that's me being mean. I'm sorry."

He laughed. "If that's as mean as you can get, it's just a butterfly fluttering her wings in reverse. Don't you worry about it."

She snorted. "Oh, I can get really mean," she declared, "but I try not to."

"Good. How's Mateo doing?" he asked suddenly.

"He's fine. Does he really help build houses for vets?" she asked.

"Yes, he does."

"He mentioned something about maybe looking at doing more of that work."

"Yeah, we were set to have a conversation about it when my wife interfered and sent him out on this job," Badger shared, with a note of humor. "We've been dealing with these War Dogs for a long time, and she thought maybe Mateo should head to your corner of the woods and see if he could help out."

"What, as a test to see if he should do more building? That's a weird test."

"Not as a test, just as somebody who could help out. He's all heart, that guy."

"I know," Maraya said. "He's been extremely supportive. I, for one, appreciate you letting him come here after the dog. He's found Thorny. I just don't know if that means Mateo's leaving right away."

"I don't see him leaving right away because he's also very

adept at dealing with vets, and it is quite possible that he's looking to help Carlos, who's struggling right now."

"You guys really seem to think Carlos is alive and he's holding the family hostage."

"I don't know if that's exactly it or not," Badger conceded, "but I can tell you it's definitely possible."

"Right," she muttered. "It could be worse."

"If you're interested in learning more about Mateo," Badger replied in a teasing tone, "you should come to New Mexico."

"New Mexico," she repeated. "I have no clue where to go, but I sure won't follow him to New Mexico based on having met him for all of five minutes."

Badger laughed. "True, yet you know more about him already than a lot of the people in that town you live in," he noted, "or the people you would have called your friends up until today."

"You could be right there," she grumbled.

"Something to think about."

"I don't have any destination in mind yet, except warmer, and I don't know what the teaching situation would be like in your corner of the world either," she murmured. "However, I would love to be involved with helping people."

"That's what we do here," Badger declared cheerfully. "We help others because somebody always needs something. Think about it, and we'll talk later." And, with that, he ended the call.

"Wait," she said into the phone, but he was gone.

What the hell was she supposed to do about setting a price for her property? It made no sense at the moment to even get an assessment with graffiti painted all over her house. Just then, she heard a vehicle from a short distance away. She bolted to her feet and ran to the front door, thinking that maybe it was Mateo and the guys. But she saw no sign of them. The vehicle stopped just up the road, and then the lights shut off. "Shit," she muttered.

She quickly grabbed her jacket and her purse, and, on second thought, ran upstairs and grabbed up a little envelope that she always kept for important personal documents—her passport and birth certificate, plus a little bit of cash. Then she bolted downstairs and out the rear kitchen door, running nonstop into the night.

She stopped when she ran out of breath. She turned, heard a *whoosh*, and suddenly her entire house went up in flames. She stood there, fumbling with her phone as she tried to talk to Badger, but her tears were interfering.

"Hang on. Hang on. What's the matter?" he cried out.

"Fire, fire! My house is on fire." She burst into sobs. "They torched it."

"Did you see who?" he asked.

She cried so hard that it was almost impossible to talk to him until she got herself under control. "No, no, no. I heard a vehicle come to a stop at the top of the hill. When they turned off the lights, I grabbed a few things and bolted out the back and ran. All I heard was a *whoosh*, and then the house just went up in flames."

MATEO SLOWLY STOOD up, raising his hands, not turning around to face the man. "Carlos, if that's you, I'm worried about your son, Timmy."

"What about him?" Carlos asked, the fear evident in his tone.

"I wanted you to know that we took him to the hospital, but, so far, he hasn't woken up." Silence came from behind him. "Did he fall? Did something happen? You've got to help me, Carlos. The doctors need to know more about what happened to him."

"I don't know," he replied, his voice thick with tears.

"You don't know, or you don't remember? There's a difference." Mateo was shoved roughly forward.

"I don't know," he snapped. "I didn't hurt my boy."

"No, maybe you didn't," Mateo acknowledged, "but I know you get headaches, and I think you forget about what's going on in your world. And then when you do remember—or can't quite remember—you're afraid a lot of times. You're afraid you did do something to your boy."

Dead silence came, and Mateo slowly turned to see an older man, looking as if he had been through many wars and hadn't ever left the battleground. He looked exhausted, as if the attempt to keep his brain sane and everything else functioning was just too much to handle.

Mateo nodded at him. "I'm not here to hurt you, Carlos. I'm not here to hunt you. I'm here to help." He waited a second as the other man just stared at him, an odd look in his black eyes. "I need to know that your wife and your daughter are okay," he began. "Emily and Donna, right?"

"Why wouldn't they be?" Carlos asked, his hand twitching on the stock of the rifle he held.

"Because you took them away from the comforts of the house."

"Bad house, bad town. Don't like anything about it. Not safe there."

After what Mateo had seen in terms of the way Maraya had been treated, he was inclined to agree. "And is it better out here?" he asked, with a slight gentle hand motion to the world around them.

"No liars here."

Mateo nodded at that. "I agree with you there. Mother Nature is at her best out here," he noted, "but it's also a hard living."

"We're fine," Carlos stated briskly.

"You aren't fine. The children aren't fine. Timmy is not fine."

At that, Carlos narrowed his gaze, apparently with a little bit of confusion, but it was so hard to see in the dark. And just then, in the background behind Mateo, he saw a light in the sky that made his heart run cold. "Good God," he gasped.

Fearing a trick, Carlos glared at him.

Mateo shook his head. "I think the house is on fire."

"Good—bad house."

"No, not your house," Mateo clarified. "Your neighbor's." He wanted to run, but, if he did, there was a good chance he would get shot just for having scared Carlos. Mateo faced him and explained, "Look. I need to go back to the house and ensure Maraya is okay. Remember Maraya?"

Carlos frowned.

"Maraya is your neighbor. She wanted to see what happened to you. She's been worried about you."

"Nobody worries," Carlos muttered. "Nobody cares. Nobody helps."

"But you don't want help, do you?" Mateo asked, staring at him, knowing that to back down at any point in time would be something that could kill him. At the same time, his heart was in his throat as he watched the sky light up with flames and smoke. From the location, he knew it would be Maraya's place. And, dear God, if she was still inside that house when it went up, no way she would have survived.

In the distance, he heard an owl. Immediately the rifle came up, and Carlos turned in a slow circle, barely taking his eyes off Mateo in order to do a quick search.

"Yes, those are my men," Mateo confirmed. "You know it. I know it, but we're not here to hurt you. You don't need to worry about it. They will not hurt you."

"Yes, they will," Carlos argued. "You want to take us away, kick us out of our home."

"Did somebody try to kick you out of your home?" he asked.

Carlos looked at him, a crazed expression on his face. "You did."

"No," Mateo declared. "I did not. I only arrived here a couple days ago. You vacated your home about ten days ago, right?"

A sound came nearby, and the little girl popped up. "Daddy?" she asked.

Carlos glared at her. "Go back down."

She hesitated. She looked over at Mateo and mouthed, *Please help*.

Again it was so shadowy and so dark, Mateo wasn't sure what he was supposed to do, but he could tell that the little girl did not want to go back, did not want to be here with her father.

Mateo turned to her father and asked, "Is this what you want for your children, to be scared all the time?"

"They're not scared. I'm keeping them safe," Carlos said gruffly. "It's not safe at the house. Bad people in town."

"Yes," Mateo agreed. "I'm not arguing with that. Bad people are here. People who don't care. People who would hurt other people, but I'm not one of them."

Carlos glared at him again. And then, hearing a sound that disturbed him, Carlos immediately crouched, lifted the rifle, and roared, "You brought the enemy! You are the enemy!" Just as he went to fire, Carlos was tackled from behind and flattened to the ground. Mateo immediately joined his buddies, and they subdued Carlos, who was even now spitting out fire and fury, but he was restrained and couldn't hurt anybody.

Mateo turned to look for the little girl, but she was gone.

CHAPTER 11

"**D**EAR GOD," MATEO grumbled into his phone as he spoke to Badger, with Jacks and Jacob and Thorny standing guard over Carlos. "They burned down her house? This is unbelievable."

"I know," Badger agreed. "So, stay calm, but we need to get Maraya."

"The guys will drop me off. They've got Carlos restrained. We need a pickup for him. He needs a medical facility, and he needs to get some help, lots of it."

"Got it," Badger noted. "I'll get back to you in a few minutes on that. And the rest of Carlos's family?"

"We've got Timmy's mother and sister, and they need to get checked out at the hospital, but I'm afraid of leaving them here alone. Somebody came to their house and basically triggered Carlos into this behavior." When he explained it to Badger, he was swearing.

"I wonder if it was those two deputies."

"I have no idea," Mateo admitted. "While the deputies are racist as hell, this would be a little bit much."

"They may not have known exactly what they were dealing with either."

"Maybe not, but I don't think they cared. For Carlos to take off with his kids and his wife like that? In his head, he was only helping them."

"I know. I understand. We all do," Badger noted, "but you need to find Maraya—now."

With that, Mateo looked at the other two, and they nodded. "Go get her. If you want, we can come with you."

"No, just drop me off closer to her house," Mateo replied. "Then you two go ahead and take Carlos and his family to the hospital."

Jacks nodded. "Hopefully her vehicle isn't burned to the ground too, but, if it is, we will deal with it," he added. "Get in. Your hands are full already."

With everybody loaded into their vehicle, Mateo looked at Emily and said, "Go see Timothy in the hospital. He needs you right now."

With tears in her eyes, she nodded. "Please help Maraya."

"I am. I'm on my way."

And, with that, Jacks dropped off Mateo in the woods closer to the burning house, as Mateo searched for Maraya on foot.

MARAYA WAS BEHIND a copse of trees, shaking with anger now.

Just then her phone buzzed. She checked, and, sure enough, a text from Badger notified her that Mateo was on his way and was looking for her. She continued filming the fire and streaming it live, which was the only thing she could figure out to do as she waited. She sent Mateo a message, asking if he was coming, and he responded immediately, texting that he was at the back of her property, heading toward her.

She carefully looked around and saw him coming to her from the woods and threw herself into his arms. It took her some time to calm down, and, when she did, she remembered why he went into the woods in the first place, and she panicked. "What about Emily and Donna?"

"They're fine. Jacob and Jacks have them. They will drop off Emily and Donna at the hospital, then may take Carlos to a medical facility where they can help him. He was stuck in the war zone. Badger's working on finding a military placement."

She sighed in relief. "So, they are all okay then?"

"Yes. Carlos was triggered by something, and people can do crazy things when they are not in their right state of mind. Badger will ensure that Carlos gets the help he needs."

"What about Thorny? What'll happen to him now that the family's so up in the air? Who'll look after him?"

Mateo shrugged. "I will probably keep him."

She looked at him, and her smile bloomed. "Aha, and I thought you weren't a softie."

"I didn't say I *wasn't* a softie," he protested. "I'm just not that much of a softie."

"Yeah, you are," she countered, with a headshake. She turned and looked back at her house, still burning bright in the sky. "I don't even hear the fire department," she whispered.

"No, I'm pretty sure we'll find out that they aren't being told, or they're all busy or something," he muttered.

Just then came the sound of sirens, heading their way.

She turned to him and frowned. "Or maybe the social media outrage has spurred their cooperation."

"I don't think everybody in town is bad," he noted, "although you've definitely had a shitty experience. So we do have to give the rest of them a pass."

She laughed, her tears still flowing. "Maybe this time, but only this time."

He turned to her and asked, "You do remember why the house is on fire, right?"

She paled, having completely put it out of her mind, and then nodded. "Yeah," she murmured. She wrapped her arms around her chest, as he put an arm around her and tucked her up close.

"If you can," he began, "say goodbye to your home right now. We'll have to talk to the officials here soon."

"I don't know why we're always talking to officials, and yet they're not doing anything to help," she complained, then gave herself a headshake. "It doesn't matter. Obviously it's a completely different game now."

CHAPTER 12

MARAYA STARED AT the local fire chief, who walked closer, his hat in his hands.

He asked her, "We do need some information to get on with our investigations."

"Yeah, well, you can ask the asshole who started the fire."

He looked at her. "Did you see who it was?"

She gave a broken laugh. "They parked on the hill and cut their lights," she stated. "As soon as I saw that, I knew it was somebody up to no good. So I grabbed a few things and bolted out the back of the house. Within minutes, I heard a weird *whoosh* sound, and the house just went up in flames."

He stared at her for a long moment. "But you didn't see anybody."

She raised her eyebrows. "If you're asking, Chief, if I stuck around while an arsonist was busy doing his thing so I could catch sight of his face, no. I was a whole lot more concerned about making sure I got out alive."

"But you have no way of knowing that's what he was planning, or did you?"

She just stared at him and didn't even bother answering. With a snort, she turned to Mateo. "I really do think it's time to leave. I can't handle staying here much longer."

He immediately nodded, put an arm around her shoulders again, and walked her back toward her truck which, thankfully, somebody had moved out of the way.

She looked up at the vehicle and asked, "I didn't even move it, did I?"

"No, I did."

"And the keys?"

"Didn't need keys," Mateo replied, with a smile. "It's a standard. Once you put it into Neutral, it just rolls. I can roll it back. Thankfully it was on a little bit of a slope. Do you have your keys?" he asked her.

She nodded, holding up the shoulder purse she still had around her neck. "Basically it's all I've got left."

"No worries. Wheels are what we need, so, for the time being, we'll take it." He turned back to the fire chief, part of the volunteer fire department for the entire county, and announced, "If you want us, we'll be over at the motel." He named the one where his buddies were staying.

The fire chief nodded. "You do know that she's, … you know, had a difficult time."

"I do know that," Mateo declared. "I also know that she was sectioned against her will and that the doctors found nothing wrong with her."

The fire chief frowned at that, staring down at the ground. "Sometimes we don't really know what's wrong with people until something happens."

"You mean, like this? Meaning, she would have torched her own home? No, Chief," Mateo snapped, "that wasn't her. You do your thing, and we will be out of your hair while you do it."

The chief stared at him, yet didn't say anything more.

Mateo nodded. "I get it. You don't want to hear anything bad about anybody in your town, but a whole lot is wrong here, and believe me that a lot of investigations are about to start."

"Is that a threat?" asked the fire chief.

"Not at all. Just letting you know. Maraya didn't do this. I have a pretty good idea who did, but I'm not telling you until we have a whole lot more information because I'm not sure you're on her side at all."

"I'm not on anybody's side," he protested.

"But you're also not a licensed arson investigator, are you?"

"No, we don't have the budget money for that."

"Somebody in this world does, and *they* will start an investigation."

Just then, another vehicle pulled up, and a man Mateo didn't recognize stepped out, walked toward the fire, stood with his hands on his hips, then looked around until he saw the fire chief. He walked over and asked, "You're managing this one?"

The fire chief nodded. "Yes. Who are you?"

"James Walder, arson investigator," he declared. "I do like to be on the scene before the embers get cold."

"We don't have arson investigators in town. I am Fire Chief Frank Lawson. We haven't even determined if it was arson."

"Not your job," he stated, turning to look at Mateo and Maraya. "Are you the owner?" he asked of Maraya.

She stepped forward from the truck and nodded. "Yes." And she relayed what she knew about what had happened. Meanwhile, the fire chief was obviously trying to get James's attention to make his impressions known too. As it was, nobody was too interested in listening to Frank's version of events. Mateo turned to the arson investigator and added,

"You need to know that at least some of the people here will suggest that she set her own house on fire, regardless of the facts."

The arson investigator stared at him for a long moment, then turned and frowned at the fire chief, who was now kicking the ground around him. "Is that true?"

"It's just one of the facts," Chief Lawson began, "that she has a history of mental instability."

At that, she cried out. "I do not! If it wasn't for my ex-husband being in a position of power, setting me up to be committed, none of that would have happened at all."

At that, James replied, "None of that has anything to do with me. I was brought in as a neutral party to ensure that everything's on the up-and-up as to this particular investigation. I will find out who set the fire and how it was set, and we'll go from there." He looked back at Mateo. "You guys will be in town?"

"We'll be in town at the motel," he stated and provided the name of the place but not the number.

James nodded. "We'll talk." And, with that, he started circling the fire.

Maraya looked over at the fire chief and snapped, "How could you even say that?" When he flushed and looked down at the ground, she stomped back to her vehicle with Thorny at her side.

Chief Lawson looked at Mateo. "You haven't known her for very long, but she's had a pretty rough life, and an awful lot of shit has gone on in her world."

"I do know that," Mateo confirmed. "And you should know that her ex-husband has also committed a lot of crimes against her in the name of love, jealousy, and just because he could, because he had the power," he pointed out. "I already hear which side you've picked, and that's fine. You don't know all the details, or maybe you don't care about the details. I do, and Maraya does. At some point in time, she will be exonerated," he stated. "This isn't just restricted to your town anymore. We've already broadcast the truth for half the world to see."

"Is she the one who caused that social media storm?" he asked, staring back at her in the truck. "That ain't gonna go over well."

"Why not? She didn't feel as if anybody here would listen to her, since you all come with your preconceived ideas, and not a one of you seems to care enough to seek the truth."

"We care," Frank blustered. "I mean, obviously she needs to be hospitalized and get the help she needs," he noted, looking at Mateo. "We don't treat our people poorly here."

Mateo shook his head and snorted. "No point in talking to you." He turned and headed back toward the truck.

"Don't leave town," the chief called out.

"You don't have the authority to tell me to do that," Mateo called back.

"No, but the sheriff does."

Mateo turned. "Chief, I really doubt that your Sheriff Riley will have the time for me. Trust me that he won't be saying anything to me about this." And, with that, he got into the truck, turned on the engine, and backed out.

"Did he just threaten you with the sheriff?" she asked, her temper boiling over.

"He did," Mateo confirmed, with a smile. "The sheriff has been the law around here for a long time, not necessarily good law, but he's the law that they know and understand. He fits what they think is good."

"Sure," she muttered, "but they're wrong."

"Don't bother arguing with them. You'll never change somebody else's opinion here," he stated. "I'm upset for you about this house, but since it was the one thing holding you back from moving on, I'm not horribly upset." He shook his head. "The transitioning will be tough, and I get that, and I'm so sorry. The memories and the PTSD that could come from something like this could be awful, and I'm horrified for you," he added. "However, the end result with a move and a fresh start will also be very good for you."

"Yeah, well, it's not as if I'll sell my house now, will I?" she said bitterly. "Who would ever want this place with it burned to the ground?"

"You still have the land." When she just shook her head, he added, "Let other people worry about that."

"Other people," she repeated, staring at him. "My world doesn't contain other people."

"It does now," he declared cheerfully, as he drove down the road.

"I don't even know why I hopped into the passenger side," she stated, staring at him. "I always drive."

"In this case, I didn't have to move you out of the driver's seat, so that saved us an argument. You're too distraught over all this. We can pick up my truck later. I don't want you alone or driving right now."

She settled into the passenger seat, not wanting to admit that he was right, but it was hard to see it any other way. When she realized they were in town, she asked, "Are we going to the hospital?"

"Do you want to go to the hospital?" he asked.

"I would like to see that Timmy is okay."

"We haven't heard anything suggesting he isn't okay. I

would imagine that he's fine, but, if you want to, we can swing by the hospital."

"I'm concerned about the whole family," she whispered.

"Then let's make a quick stop."

As they walked through the hospital parking lot with Thorny at her side, she looked at the War Dog and noted, "He didn't like Chief Lawson."

"Yeah, but he liked James well enough," he said with a smirk, mentioning the arson investigator.

"Apparently Thorny has good taste then, doesn't he?" she replied, grinning broadly.

He laughed. "He does, indeed." He bent to stroke Thorny on the head. As they walked inside the hospital, Alex sat at the front desk, looked up, saw them, and frowned. Then she dropped her gaze to the desk in front of her.

Mateo walked straight up to the reception desk. "Hi, Alex." She just nodded. "Will we have a problem?"

She raised her eyebrows and shook her head. "I don't think so, unless you're planning on causing trouble."

He laughed. "You're the one who frowned when you saw us."

She immediately got flustered. "It's just we've heard some strange stories tonight."

"You mean, how Maraya's house was torched by an arsonist?"

"Or by someone," she clarified immediately and then flushed.

"Wow, it doesn't take long for nasty gossip to crawl in here, does it?" Maraya stated, staring at this woman she had known for some time, whose young daughter attended the school where Maraya had taught.

Alex flushed again. "You can't bring the dog in here,"

she finally said.

"Yes, I certainly can," Mateo countered.

"No, I was told to warn you that the dog isn't allowed inside."

"Really, and who told you that?" he asked.

"My boss," she said, looking at him in confusion. "It's not me. I'm only passing on what I've been told."

Mateo stepped away, taking Maraya with him, as he pulled out his phone and immediately called Badger. "So, we're being refused entrance to the hospital with Thorny."

"That's nice," Badger noted. "Give me a minute."

Maraya looked over at Mateo. "I only heard part of that."

"He's gone off to make the appropriate phone calls."

"I thought it was already settled."

"It is, but sometimes, no matter where you are, some people always think they know better and should get to make the rules, instead of listening to others who have the right to make the rules."

"Does Badger really have a connection to the hospital?"

"Kat does. She's one of the top prosthetic designers in the country. This is the work she does, remember? And, beyond that, they are connected to quite a few other people involved in hospital work."

Just then, a man came down the hallway, his white jacket flapping behind him, an earnest expression on his face. He gave them a genial and obviously fake smile. "Hey, Maraya. How are you doing? I heard the news. That's terrible."

She nodded. "It's been a pretty-rough day."

"I'm sure it has," he agreed immediately. He turned to Mateo, and his smile chilled. "I understand that you're looking to see Timothy Martinez."

"Yes, we have come to check up on the family," he shared in a mild tone. "Your receptionist is denying us access."

"It's not that I'm denying you access," she snorted. "I'm denying the dog access." She looked down at Thorny in disgust. "We shouldn't have animals in the hospital."

"Now, now, that's all right, dear," the administrator replied. "He does have clearance, so he will be allowed to see the child."

Alex stared at him in astonishment. "But, Dr. Gilbert, you told me earlier that nobody was allowed and definitely not the dog."

"Yes, I did, but things have changed." Dr. Gilbert glanced hesitantly over at the visitors.

Mateo nodded. "Yeah, cuts to your budget have a way of doing that, I suppose."

He flushed and shook his head. "Now, no need for that kind of talk. Please make your visit without any issues and leave peacefully."

"We never intended to do anything else," Mateo declared. He nodded at the receptionist, as Maraya tucked her hand in his, and they walked down the hallway, Thorny between them.

"What the hell kind of pull does this Badger guy have?" she asked him.

"It's not even so much that he has any pull. It's just the connections, both private and government, and let's face it. Money talks, or I suspect it's the threat of no money that did the talking here. That kind of thing can make it easier to do what needs to be done," he shared, "and let's face it, no reason for them to deny the dog."

"It is a hospital," she pointed out.

"Sure, but this has nothing to do with the dog himself and everything to do with the people here and their piss-poor attitudes. Which is why it's so damn poisonous and why you need to get out."

"Right, well, apparently I'm getting out no matter what because I don't have any way to stay now, even if I wanted to," she snapped. "My house burned down tonight. Remember?"

Mateo stopped at a door and opened it and stepped inside. Sure enough, there was Timmy, and seated off to the side was his mother, Emily Martinez, and his sister, Donna, was curled up in another chair, sleeping.

Emily hopped to her feet and raced forward, wrapping her arms around Maraya. "Thank you so much," she whispered.

Maraya gave her a big hug and looked at her, tears in her eyes. "I couldn't believe it when you guys just up and left."

"Not by choice either," she muttered, "but Carlos—he's just not the same man anymore." She looked over at Mateo. "Where did they take him?"

"He's been taken to a hospital for assessment."

Her face fell. "I guess I know what that means."

"Yes and no. It's not as if he'll be locked up if he doesn't need to be. I guess it depends on if you want to press charges, if he was holding you all against your will."

She immediately shook her head. "No, he was just trying to help in his way. He thought he was keeping us safe."

Mateo smiled at her. "In his mind, that is exactly what he was doing. It could have been much worse out there. He could have shot us, but he didn't."

"And thank God for that," she whispered, shaking her head. "It's so hard to have him around when he's unstable.

Do you really think they can do something to help him?"

"I'm sure there is," Mateo replied, "but it won't be an instant solution. It might take some time to work out proper medications and the right therapy, but there is hope."

She smiled up at him. "That's very good to hear. My mother wants us to move back to her area and away from here. I don't know whether that's a good thing or not right now. How long do you think his treatment will be?" She looked over at him and back at Maraya.

Mateo sighed. "It'll be a while, and he might be better off in another location too."

She nodded. "People have been acting really strange around him and seemed to set him off all the time. It's not even so much *strange* as," she clarified hesitantly, "they just haven't been very nice."

"Have you been having trouble in town?" Maraya asked.

"We get racist comments a lot anyway," she noted. "Most of the time we just ignore it. It's been hard on the kids, but, for whatever reason, it's just gotten really abusive." Emily sighed, her shoulders sinking. "That's why I was thinking it would be nice to get a fresh start."

"I would do it," Maraya stated, and then she winced. "It's not as if I have a choice. I'll be getting a new start too."

Emily stared at her in confusion.

"Somebody just torched my house."

Emily's hand slapped against her mouth, and she gasped. "Oh my God." She glanced at Mateo, now back to Maraya. "And you're sure it was arson?"

She nodded. "Yes, and it's a good thing Carlos was being picked up at the time because otherwise somebody would have tried to blame him."

Emily immediately nodded. "I know. Gosh, it's hard to

find anything to be grateful for in our situation, but that is definitely a start." She turned to Mateo. "Thank you so much for helping us."

Mateo just smiled, looking down at Thorny, who still sat at his side.

Emily then addressed Thorny. "And thank you, Thorny, for saving my Timmy. I just didn't know what else to do, but, when Carlos saw you out there, he was getting so irate and so scared. So I just told him that, if you took Timmy away, then our son could get the help he needed, and everybody would leave us alone. I think he only believed me because somewhere in his mixed-up mind was the knowledge that Timmy really needed help." Emily glanced back at her son in the hospital bed. "And the good news is, he woke up earlier."

"Oh, that's wonderful news," Maraya said, as she walked closer to the bed. Timmy was sleeping soundly at the moment, but it was a restful sleep. "The fact that he's woken up is massive."

"Yes, and, as soon as he's back on his feet"—she glanced at the two of them—"I think my mother's place will be a great choice for us."

Maraya asked, "What about Carlos? Do you want him back when this all blows over?"

"I'm hoping that maybe we can find a way to get him away from here," she explained. "I have been talking to some people, hoping they can help. This will never be a good place for him."

"That's obvious," Mateo said. "I might be able to help with that."

She looked at him and shook her head. "You've already done so much."

"There's no limit on how much anybody can help," he replied. "So, if I can do a little more, I will."

She smiled. "Thank you. You've been a godsend already. I don't know what I would have done if we'd stayed out there much longer."

"Hopefully you would have gotten away somehow," Mateo suggested. "If you don't mind my asking, what really happened to Timmy?"

"Carlos hit him. He didn't mean to, and Timmy fell backward and hit his head on a rock," she shared, again turning back to her son. "I didn't know how to help him. There was nothing I could do out there. Carlos wouldn't let me leave, wouldn't let me go see anybody, wouldn't let me take Timmy anywhere. Carlos is just not right in his mind, and I know he needs help," she admitted. "Maybe now he can finally get it."

"I think so," Mateo replied, "but I think it's also why it'll take time for him to heal and to get to the point where he can see you guys on a regular basis."

She nodded. "If it can be close enough that I can drive to him, that's fine," she noted. "We will make the trip to see him. No matter what others may say, he is their father and my husband, and he is a good man," she stated defiantly.

MATEO KNEW WHAT Emily meant. He'd seen it time and time again, and she was right. On the one side, Carlos was a good man. He was just doing what he believed he needed to do to save his family. On the other hand, he was an irresponsible father who put his family in harm's way. Therein lays the real crux of the issue.

Carlos was confused, tired, worn out, and needed some time to heal and rest, just like so many others who came back from war, completely at odds with the world around them. Things had changed so much, and sometimes in ways that they couldn't even comprehend. Sadly far too many people could only see it through tainted glass, forgetting the sacrifice and service to his country that put Carlos in that position to begin with.

Emily turned to Maraya. "And now your house—what will you do?"

She shook her head. "I don't know. I was talking about selling it and maybe had somebody who was interested, at least until it burned to the ground," she added sadly. "Now I don't know. It is insured, but you know what that's like."

"I do know," Emily muttered. "Oftentimes we couldn't even get insurance. So many years we didn't have any insurance, medical or otherwise, just because it's so expensive." She looked back at Mateo. "If I give you our new address, will you find out if there's any way that we can move my husband closer to us?"

"It will be out of my hands as to where he is placed," Mateo explained, "but I can let you know if there is a center or something close by."

She immediately gave him the address of her mother's house.

Mateo smiled. "I'll pass it on. That's all I can do."

She nodded. "I understand. Anything you can do will be appreciated. I don't want to see him here. It's this place, this town, that sent him into such a spiral already."

"Got it," he said. "I'm not sure any of you will want to stay here after this."

"Yes," Maraya agreed, turning to him. "Everybody who's

here now, well, they will see me as the bad guy. They won't see the sheriff as anything other than doing what he was entitled to do."

"Jesus," Mateo muttered.

Emily asked her, "Is he still hitting you?"

"No," she stated, turning back to her with a smile. "Although he did think about trying again."

"I would love to see you away from here too," Emily shared warmly. "After what they did to you? It was all terrible." She looked back at Mateo. "They planned to lock her away in a mental institute and throw away the key. That's just not fair."

He nodded, but then asked, "Did you hear that from her?"

"No, I heard them talking about it at a restaurant, the deputies, Rodney and Xavier, and the sheriff. I was there to get work, cleaning for meals basically," she explained. "We were really struggling at the time, and they were sitting in a corner, talking about her. It was pretty bad."

"Any chance you would be prepared to put that in a statement?"

"Yes, of course. Why?"

"Because that is criminal activity, and Riley shouldn't be allowed to get away with that. There wasn't any sign that she needed to have that kind of treatment, and the doctors did release her because she was totally fine. But still, it went on her record."

"I know. They were making it out to be that she was suicidal—or at least that's what their plan was," Emily shared. "I'd never seen any sign of that with her, but I didn't know her all that well," she added apologetically, "but they were talking about it."

"If you can write down just what you heard, that would be a help," Mateo stated. "Any ammunition we have against the treatment she's been given will help a lot."

"Not an issue," Emily replied. "After what you've done for us, I'm more than happy to help."

"Just put down the truth though," Maraya added. "Don't embellish it, just the truth."

She laughed. "What I heard was plenty bad enough. It doesn't need any embellishing."

Maraya winced. "And that's the problem with exes. They tend to get very vindictive."

"I can't believe you were even married to him," she muttered. "I mean, he is one unhappy man."

Maraya nodded. "He isn't happy at all. I just don't know if he's murderously unhappy."

"There was some talk about money," Emily added, frowning at her. "I thought maybe you had money and that, if you were committed, he would get control of it somehow."

"I don't think so," Maraya said, shaking her head, "but then maybe I need to go visit the lawyer's office too."

"What lawyer?" Mateo asked. "You told me that no one was in town who would be fair, and you even had to go a town over to look for a divorce attorney."

"It's the old lawyer that my family used, and I know that at one point in time Riley was trying to get a hold of the family home."

"He shouldn't have been able to do anything about that legally, if it was all taken care of."

"Sure, but we were husband and wife, remember? At one point in time, he also tried to get me sectioned because I was uncooperative as a wife."

"Emily snorted. "Yeah, well, there are a couple other

names for that attitude too."

She looked over at her and smiled. "That's the thing. You know when you're in a district where men are of the opinion that they're superior and can do anything they want, it's pretty hard to fight them."

"And you shouldn't have to," Emily said, staring at her, "any more than I should have been out in the woods trying to protect the kids by cooperating, but the men are the physically stronger ones of the partnership. So, sometimes, when they are out of control, they don't care and just want everybody else to pay." She turned back to Timmy and stroked his shoulder. "I just need to know that he'll be okay, and then we're out of here," she shared. "My mother and my brother are already coming to pack up what is left at the house."

"There wasn't much," Maraya noted. "It was left in pretty rough shape."

"Yeah, I know, but the kids need clothes. If anything's salvageable, I would like to get a few personal items if I can." Her gaze glanced at her daughter. "Although a clean break might be better. Sometimes all that stuff just becomes baggage."

Thorny growled ever-so-slightly and immediately stepped back, only to have his demeanor immediately turn to something much happier. Mateo opened the hospital room door, and his two friends, Jacks and Jacob, walked in.

They both smiled at him. "We heard you had trouble getting in here."

"Yes," he confirmed, then introduced them to Emily, who immediately gave them both hugs with effusive thanks.

The men, slightly uncomfortable, stepped back, and Jacks asked, "You're staying here, ma'am, with your son?"

She nodded. "My daughter is asleep here too, and I'm not sure where else I can go. My brother will be here tomorrow, with our mother, and they're coming to help pack me up and move me to my mother's house," she explained.

"Good," Jacks replied, with a smile.

Maraya looked over at them. "Did something change?"

"Nope," Jacob stated cheerfully. "Nothing's changed."

But she wasn't so sure.

The newcomers looked at Mateo, and Jacks asked, "May we speak with you outside?"

He immediately nodded, looked over at her, and said, "I'll be right back."

She watched with a frown as they stepped out into the hallway, but she turned back and gave Emily a reassuring smile. "It's all right. These are the good guys."

Mateo, hearing that last bit, smiled as he stepped out into the hallway, Thorny at his side, closing the door behind him. "What's up?"

As the two men stood here in the hallway, Thorny was busy greeting them, getting as many cuddles and pets as he could.

Mateo smiled at his antics. "This dog is very friendly," he noted, with a laugh, "although he growled when you approached the door just now, then immediately recognized friend from foe."

"Good," Jacks said. "We talked to Badger and James, the arson investigator, who stated it was definitely arson and what Maraya noted sounds right. Incendiaries were thrown at the house."

"So, it was exactly as she said, a sudden *whoosh*?"

"Yes," Jacob confirmed, with a nod. "Thank God she

wasn't inside. We are also of the opinion that she could still be in danger."

"Which is why I'm sticking close to her," Mateo declared. "So, what are you guys doing now?"

"We're not at all sure that the family is safe either. Carlos Martinez was the hazard before, but Jacob and I, we just want to ensure that the family is okay too. So we thought we would stick around here, so that you guys could go to the motel and could get a bit of a break."

"Except, if they know we're at the motel, I don't know if that's safe either."

"And that's a good point too," Jacks seconded. "The investigator is sending his report, and they've gone over the sheriff's head."

"They have to when he's potentially involved in the whole thing."

"Exactly, and his deputies."

Jacob added, "I wish we had some way of knowing who started the fire."

Mateo pointed out, "Maraya watched as the vehicle stopped at the top of the hill, and I'm betting there are tracks. That would be at least something."

Jacks nodded. "If you want to go back out and get them, we could do this one man at a time, or two can go, as long as everyone stays here together with one of us. At least one of us should be here at all times."

"Why don't you guys do that—one get the tire prints and the other stay with the family," Mateo suggested. "I'll take Maraya to the motel, get her to crash for at least a little bit, if I can. She's stressed out now, but, once that adrenaline wears off, which we're getting pretty close to, she'll need to drop and then recover."

"Badger is of the opinion that she's definitely not safe going forward and suggested she make a relocation plan very quickly."

"Sure, but he also had a potential buyer arranged for her house. Now that it's burned down, that's a whole different deal."

"Oh, that's the other thing. Sorry. Badger spoke to the possible buyer about the fire. Turns out he didn't want the house anyway. He's just after the land, so the deal is still on."

"He knows the house is in total shambles?"

"Yes, that's what the new deal is. It's for the land, and he's hoping that she has insurance for the house. Social media's in an uproar, so quite a stink is happening, and a lot of people are following it now."

"Good," Mateo stated. "I'm not big on social media, but, if it brought her some well-deserved respite from all these intimidation tactics, that's a good thing."

"Also a federal investigation is going on about her being sectioned," Jacks added. "So definitely some people need to talk to her."

"I'm not sure she'll want to press charges."

"Maybe not, but it's also a case of abuse of power all around. Riley and his racist deputies have been operating without any regard for her rights, using his position as sheriff, coupled with his abusive nature." Jacks smiled. "This stuff is all stirred up, and now we need to ensure the follow-through happens, and Riley can never be a sheriff again."

"That will be great, but I'm not even sure that's enough."

"Nope, neither are we, neither is Badger, but let's start with what we can get."

Mateo grimaced, looking at his two buddies. "She has

mentioned some things about the way her fiancé, Riley's brother, suddenly died after the accident, when it was thought he would survive his injuries. She has at times wondered if Riley had something to do with that."

"Because of Maraya?"

"Plus, it may have been about her family's farm. I don't think Riley was the sheriff yet. His brother was about to marry Maraya, and they had a son on the way."

"So, he just wanted his brother's life, is that it?" Jacks asked.

"I don't know for certain, but I think it bears checking out."

"It absolutely does," Jacks agreed, with a knowing glance at Jacob. "That will be fun." He shook his head. "Man, the shit people get up to just amazes me."

The door opened then, and Maraya stepped out. "Any chance we can go crash? I'm fading fast, and I want to get out of here before I hit the ground."

"Absolutely," Mateo stated, with a smile. "I was just talking to the guys about it."

She smiled at them and asked, "Are you heading back to the motel too?"

"Nope, we'll stand watch here, at least until Emily's brother arrives."

She studied them for a long moment, took a deep slow breath, and then nodded. "That's a good idea." She glanced from one to the other. "I hope nothing else bad will happen here. They've been through enough already."

"And so have you," Jacks added, as he stepped forward and gave her a hug. "Now, you guys go crash. We'll stay on the job."

She smiled. "Not much to protect anymore," she muttered. "My house is gone."

"Yes, but the arson investigator has ruled it to be arson," he shared.

Maraya sighed. "Sure, but the locals will just say it was me. That's what Fire Chief Lawson was already trying to tell the arson investigator," she said, with a headshake. "As much as I really don't care, I do care. I care a lot, but I'm just so tired of fighting."

They nodded. "Go get some rest. We'll be right here."

And, with that, Mateo put an arm around her shoulders and nudged her toward the front entrance, Thorny at her side.

Maraya looked down at Thorny. "I did mention him to Emily."

He nodded. "And her answer was no, I presume?"

"As much as the kids love him, Emily's mother doesn't, and right now Emily has to do what's best for all of them."

"I get it. He was a dog for their father, but that doesn't mean he'll be the best choice for them to have right now, living in a multigenerational home."

"No, I don't think anybody is ready for this right now," Maraya replied. "Seems to me that you may have found yourself a new dog."

He laughed. "Can't say I'm surprised."

"I am," she said, looking over at him. "I mean, he's a great dog, but it's a huge commitment, and if you're not settled—"

"Hey, don't speak for me. I can build dog houses as well as I can build people houses," he declared, with a smile.

She studied him and then started to laugh. "I hadn't considered that."

He grinned at her. "See? Things have a way of working out."

"I wish I had your optimism," she muttered, then yawned a huge deep yawn.

He smiled. "Come on. Sleep first, then the optimism when you wake up."

"If you say so," she muttered, and he led her out to the vehicle.

CHAPTER 13

M ARAYA WOKE UP many hours later and stared around in confusion. Within seconds, everything that had gone on recently flooded her mind. She groaned at the pain of what her world had become, still unable to process the whole thing. Not teary but not far from it. When a gentle knock came on her bedroom door, she called out, "Come in."

Mateo stepped in, holding a cup of coffee.

"If that's coffee"—she rolled her eyes—"I might forgive you for all the ills of the world."

"I'm not responsible for the ills in the world," he stated, with a smile, "but it is definitely coffee."

She shuffled back up against the headboard, as he set it down on the night table. "What time it is?" she asked, looking around. "Once I closed the curtains, I was out. I was beyond tired."

"It's morning," he said, with a smile.

She stared at him in disbelief, pretty sure she'd gone to bed well before bedtime. Even with the house burning and whatnot, she'd slept through the night? "I didn't think it was possible, but I slept like a log."

"And that's how you're supposed to sleep. That's good."

She smiled as she hugged the cup of coffee. "Did you get any sleep?"

"I did," he said, looking at her with a grin on his face. "Probably better than you did."

"Probably," she muttered, followed by a dry laugh. "Although I was just so exhausted, so over it all, I'm not sure anything was functioning beyond the need to get out of there."

"Sometimes that need to get out is all there is."

"Any updates?"

Mateo nodded. "An APB is out for the good Sheriff Riley and his merry men."

She stared at him in shock. "Really?" He nodded. "Oh, good God, how the hell did that happen?"

"Both Rodney and Xavier are considered persons of interest in the arson case the feds are looking at."

"But nobody did anything overnight in terms of forensics or anything, I'm sure."

"My guys went and took tire track impressions up at the house late yesterday, right where you saw the vehicle stopped just before the fire, and it does fit the deputy's vehicle. The footprints that went down to the house also fit the deputies, but short of being able to place them there to start the fire, we do have a match for the deputies footprints. In that job, they had the legal ability to wander all over the place."

"Yes, of course, and they were definitely there earlier with their spray cans, as my first video proves," she reminded him. "So, why an APB? Is that really enough?"

"Not necessarily, but they skipped town, or so we think. No one's been able to locate them," he shared cheerfully.

"All three of them?"

"No sign of the sheriff today so far, and it appears his deputies have skipped. People are looking to talk to all of them."

"Riley won't leave," she stated. "That's not who he is. Riley will find a way to fix this."

"That would be good if he could. I mean, the investigators into this case would very much like to know just what he was involved in and how much of what he was doing was legit, versus an abuse of power," Mateo explained, with a big smile.

"That'll get me involved too, won't it?"

"They'll need to talk to you, but believe me that they'll need to talk to you regardless."

"And why is that?" she asked.

"Because there's the house to deal with and your marriage, your divorce, all that stuff."

"You should probably go subpoena the lawyer then."

"Your current lawyer? The divorce attorney?"

"No, the old family lawyer," she clarified, with a sigh. "He's the one who told me to take the money and run, and he disappeared afterward because he felt things weren't kosher. But he set up my parents' estates so that I got my inheritance. I gather against Riley's wishes. I don't know."

"Maybe Riley was just smart enough to realize that things were getting too hot here." He immediately asked for the lawyer's name and any contact information she had.

She pulled out her phone and showed him the contacts. "Grab whoever you want," she muttered. "I don't know anything anymore. So much shit has been going on for so long. I'm not sure I even know who's involved and who's not."

"There will be plenty of time to find out," he said, as he went through her contacts, found a bunch of names of interest, and started firing them off to his boss. "Badger's taking care of all this."

Maraya noted, "Badger seems to have far-reaching fingers."

"He has a lot of fingers and a lot of favors that he can pull in. He helps an awful lot of people, and there are always people in his world who want to do the right thing," he shared, looking over at her with a smile. "Believe it or not, good people are in this world too."

Her phone rang just then. She stared down and said, "I don't know this number."

He answered it for her, stating that it was her phone. There was a surprised moment on the other end, and then the person replied, "I am Mark Slinger. I was looking to buy her property. Is she even around?"

"She is, indeed. Hang on." Mateo handed over her phone.

Maraya listened in astonishment as Mark offered her a price that made her eyes water. "I'm sure that's way too much," she replied.

"I don't care," he declared, his tone rough. "You've been to hell and back, and these assholes have been getting away with this shit for far too long. For the longest time, I didn't give a crap. I was just on the outside looking in," he explained. "But then I started seeing how much crap they're pulling, and I just can't sit here and do nothing. So, you need a fresh start, and I can always use the land."

"My land is also connected to the land owned by the family of Carlos Martinez. They'll be looking to sell as well, if you're interested."

"Who are they?"

He sounded confused, as if he didn't know anything about it. "Have you not heard that story either?" she asked.

"No, I don't think so," he replied.

She put her phone on Speaker, and, between her and Mateo, they explained it to him.

"Ten days?" he repeated. "That guy had them out there for ten days, and nobody went looking?"

"Exactly," she confirmed.

"Jesus Christ. Fine," he said. "I need more land. That's an easy answer."

"It depends on how deep your pockets are," Mateo noted, with a laugh.

"Deep enough for this shit," he stated. "You can never have too much land."

Mateo certainly wouldn't argue with that because Slinger was right. "Emily Martinez is at the hospital right now, and I believe her brother is on his way to help them move out of here."

"Good," Mark replied. "Like everybody else, they need to get out of here and find another place to live."

"And what about you?"

"I came here to get away from people," he shared. "I burned myself out doing what I was doing, and now it seems as if maybe I found another cause to fight for," he added, a note of humor shining through the phone.

"And that's a good thing."

"So, you guys go off and do your thing, and I will contact the lawyers to set this up. However, don't tell your insurance company we have a deal."

"Why not?" she asked.

"Because they'll owe you for the house, and that's on top of what this purchase price is. Just because you might sell the land doesn't mean they get to cut your insurance settlement," he warned. "Insurance companies are notorious for being assholes. Don't let them walk all over you."

"They'll say I burned down my own house," she noted. "It was arson."

"Did you?" he asked, with a question in his voice.

"No. Of course not," she stated, staring in shock at the phone.

"Good, I didn't think so."

Maraya could almost hear the smile in his tone.

"So, you just hold firm. Let them deal with their shit, don't be in a big hurry to settle, and, at the end of the day, they'll still pay you." With that, he ended the call.

She stared at Mateo as she slowly put her phone on the bed. "Apparently—"

"I heard." He smiled. "As I mentioned, good people are in this world too."

"Yeah, but he's just buying the property for more money than its worth because he's pissed off."

"I don't care about his reason because he's doing it with his eyes wide open, and apparently he can afford it. The main thing is you'll be getting it sold and getting a fair price, so it's a good deal for you. He's a big boy, and, if he wants to pay you a good price, that's his choice. As he said, maybe he has a new cause to work on."

She smiled. "It makes sense in a way. He mentioned something about being burned out and hiding away, but now he's fired up again."

"And that's a good thing," Mateo pointed out. "Let him be fired up and do his thing, and you do yours. With any luck, it will all work out. Now, finish your coffee, grab a shower, and then I suggest we go find some food."

IT WAS ALMOST another hour before they left the motel, but she had showered and was feeling a whole lot better, even if she had to wear the same clothes.

He smiled at her as he walked them down to the street level. "We can drive somewhere, or we can just try this place across the street."

She stared across the street and shrugged. "I haven't been in there before."

"In that case, why don't we try it out?"

"Are you sure it's safe?"

"It's as safe as anywhere else. I don't know what kind of reception we'll get, but I suggest we go find out. You can't hide away from the world, and remember that you haven't done anything wrong." She winced, and he watched as her steps slowed. "We have to face the music sometime."

"Sure, but you know everybody will believe I set my own house on fire," she muttered in a frustrated tone.

"Some may, but, when they realize that Riley, Rodney, and Xavier are on the run, that may be a whole different story. If you walk right in, your head held high, you'll at least give them something to think about."

"Are they on the run though?" she asked, with a wry smile. "People talk all the time, but that doesn't mean it's the truth."

"Maybe not," Mateo conceded, "but apparently you haven't checked out your social media feeds this morning."

"No, I didn't even look."

"And that's a good thing," he said, with a cheerful smile. "Because it's still trending everywhere. There's a full investigation brewing on many levels into this lovely little town of yours. Suddenly all kinds of questions are being asked about how they handle things around here."

"Oh, *great*," she muttered. "That'll just piss off people."

"Maybe at first, yet it'll bring them some business, and things aren't exactly great around here these days, so maybe it's a good thing."

They walked into the café and immediately headed to a table in the back.

The waitress looked over at them and froze, before she came running. "You shouldn't be here," she hissed.

Mateo sat down in the booth. "Why not?" he asked casually, ignoring the waitress's flushed face.

"Because my boss is really upset." She looked over at Maraya. "Are you okay, honey?"

Maraya smiled at her. "I'm fine, except I'm really hungry. It's been a very long night."

"Of course it has. Oh, my goodness, your house. I can't believe that it burned."

"I can't either. ... I had the unfortunate job of watching it go, as everything from my family was destroyed." Even now, it choked her up.

The older woman immediately patted Maraya's hand. She glanced around and added, "The boss doesn't want you here, but I'll just say I didn't recognize you."

She laughed. "If that works for you, it works for me."

"Maybe he'll stay in his office." The waitress bustled away and came back with coffee, but she kept looking toward the back.

"Is he likely to cause a scene if we're here?" Mateo asked.

She winced and nodded. "Yes, 100 percent. One of the deputies is his son."

He stared at her and then slowly nodded. "I guess, in a town like this, everybody is connected and related, aren't they?"

"They sure are," Maraya muttered. The waitress returned, and Maraya asked her, "Do you like it here?"

"It's not the same as it was, that's for sure," the waitress replied. "My husband passed away a couple years back, and I've just been, well, it's home," she said. "I always intended to move on but never could overcome my inertia, I guess. So, I stayed, and, whether it's the right thing or not, I don't know. But things are certainly getting exciting around here now," she quipped, as she looked over at Maraya. "I'm surprised. I just figured you were this quiet little thing, and now, all of a sudden, you've become somebody everybody wants to know."

"I don't think they want to know me," she clarified, "as much as they may just want me to get lost."

"Oh, I don't know if that's it," the waitress countered, with a laugh. "Everybody's been following your social media accounts, so that's a good thing."

"Maybe." Maraya shrugged.

They ordered, and their meal came fast enough that Maraya thought the waitress was probably trying to serve them immediately get them to move on. When they were finally done eating, she got up and walked toward the front counter, a man was standing there, glaring at her.

The waitress immediately stepped between the two of them. She smiled at Maraya and said, "Thanks for coming by."

Realizing that the waitress was trying to soothe what would be troubled water, Maraya nodded and stepped toward the door, but the man had other ideas. He grabbed her arm and spun her around, only to find himself lifted into the air as Mateo got very close to his face. "Nobody puts their hands on a woman in anger, and that, my friend, is the last time you will ever touch her."

The older man sputtered, as the rest of the people sitting at the tables gasped and murmured among themselves.

The waitress hurriedly interjected, "Please let him go. He's just a foolish old man, and his son is in trouble right now."

The old man spat, "He's not in any trouble. If it wasn't for this tart, he wouldn't have any trouble at all."

"Really? You mean the son who torched my house last night?" Maraya was spitting fire. "The son who wouldn't go looking for a missing family? The son who threatened me," she added. "And let's not forget that an APB is out on your son and his buddy even as we speak."

Silence fell in the diner.

"And the sheriff too," she snapped, glaring at the old man's face. "All on the run. That's some man you raised."

He stared at her and immediately shook his head. "That's not true. There's no way. They are the law."

Maraya clarified, "They *were* the law, and they lost sight of what that meant. So, they aren't the law anymore, which is why they're on the run, because they know they're in trouble. So, good luck even hearing from your son until he's picked up and brought in for questioning. I'm sure you'll hear from him the minute he needs your help to bail him out of yet another shitty scenario."

He just glared at her and took another step forward, but instead of backing away, she shoved her face into his. "Go ahead. I've taken far too much abuse from people like you and that goddamn asshole ex-husband of mine," she exclaimed. "So many of the men in this town are just the same. If you don't get what you want, you just beat it out of everybody. The women in your lives serve as some punching bag for you abusive types," she snapped. "But your son won't get away with all the shit he's pulled. He's gone too far, so you best start worrying about bailing him out. Start gathering up your pennies so you can get him a good lawyer because he's sure as hell gonna need one."

And, with that, she turned and stormed out of the restaurant. She didn't even realize that Mateo had come outside until a hand landed on her shoulder. She immediately stiffened.

Mateo whispered, "It's all right. It's just me." She turned to glare at him, and he nodded. "That's how this will go while you are in this town, so no point in getting engaged in further arguments," he stated.

"So, what am I even here for? I might as well open a bloody map, take out a pin, and stab a location as my next place of residence," she cried out. "I've got absolutely no purpose in going anywhere. I don't have a home. I don't have a job. I don't have a family. I don't have anything." She raised both hands in surrender. "And he's sitting here, defending that piece-of-crap son of his."

"That's because he doesn't want to see who his son has really become. He's been defending him since forever because it was easier than opening his eyes to the stuff his son was up to. He wants to believe in the law, wants to believe that his son is a good boy."

"Some *boy*—"

"I get it. But, at some point, people can't keep listening to the lies, and that awakening is hard on everybody."

"Maybe so," she muttered irritably, "but it shouldn't have to be my pain too."

"No, it shouldn't," he agreed, with a smile. "And you're doing a great job of letting it go, so you can be on your own merry way."

She rolled her eyes at that. "It sure doesn't seem like it."

"You're doing fine. We just need to keep going and figure out what's next." Just then his phone rang, and he said, "This may be what's next."

"*Great*," she muttered, as she paced the parking lot. She watched as he listened to whoever was on the other end. He ended the call, then turned to her and smiled. "When you have money, you can really make things happen. The documents are ready for you to sign for the sale of your property."

She turned and stared at him in shock. "Already?"

"Yes," he confirmed.

"Even though there's an investigation?"

"Dealing with that is another one of the things we need to do today," he noted, looking around the empty lot.

"*Great*," she muttered. "I don't even know what the hell I'm supposed to do at this point. So just point me in the right direction and tell me what to do."

"No, I'm not doing that," he declared. "Nobody is telling you what to do. It's up to you to assess the options and to figure it out. You won't be forced into something you don't agree on."

She groaned. "That's not what I meant."

"I know that," he said, "but, in the mood you're in and all you've been through, we need to keep calm heads. You don't have a house anymore to sell, but, if you want to sell the property, you have an offer available, with paperwork to sign at his attorney's office here in town."

She stared at him and then nodded. "Nothing is left of that property for me. So, yes, I would like to sell it. At least the money would give me something to start with."

"It will." With that, he turned and looked around, then checked his watch. "His office should be open today, so you could sign whenever you're ready. I suggest we consider taking advantage of that."

They walked to the motel, and she went straight to her vehicle, put Thorny into the back seat, and climbed right into the driver's seat. He smiled and got in. She looked at him and asked, "No arguments?"

"Nope. Last night you weren't in any shape to drive," he shared, with a smile. "Today, it's a different story."

She groaned. "Are you always this reasonable?"

"Yes," he declared immediately.

"You know, it's damn irritating." He burst out laughing, the sound tugging a reluctant grin to her face. "It might be irritating," she admitted, "but it's also really soothing."

"I don't know about soothing, and I don't recall anyone ever saying that to me," he shared, with a smile. "But let's just see what we can knock off our to-do list. You'll also need some clothes, I presume?"

She nodded. "Yeah, I was thinking of that earlier when I got dressed. So, first the lawyers, then the bank, and then shopping." And that's what they did.

It took hours, and afterward she held up her hand and announced, "I'm done. I'm so done."

"So, where do you want to go? Either we can go back to the motel or we can go for lunch."

She thought about it. "Maybe lunch, or one better, can we pick up something and take it back to my place?"

"Your place?" he asked questioningly.

"I would like to have a picnic, you know, and say goodbye."

"You do realize that it's not yours anymore, right?"

She winced. "I guess. Do I need his permission to go there today?"

"We can ask him, but you did sell it. So, it's not technically yours anymore."

"Right," she muttered, shaking her head. "Funny how I assumed it still was."

"The sale was complete upon closing, which was complete upon signing, and in this case, possession was today. Although," he added, as he looked at his watch, "didn't it say 3:00 p.m.? We can check your copy, but I'm sure it did, in which case we have until then."

"Good," she said. "Let's go."

They quickly picked up sandwiches and some drinks, plus coffees, and she drove back to her place. It was only one o'clock, so they had a couple hours. When they got there, she stood here for a long moment, just staring at the remnants of her home.

"Good God," she mumbled. "It's pretty scary to think that I could have been in there, and, if I hadn't heard the truck and seen where they parked, I would have been."

"I think that was the intent. You were supposed to be in there."

"That's unbelievable," she said, as she stared at the devastation. Her voice got hoarse, and tears clogged her throat, as she studied the remnants of her life. "What a mess."

"It's not your mess. It's not even your problem anymore," Mateo noted. "I guess it still is in the sense that we have to deal with the insurance company, but it's no longer an issue in terms of your having to deal with it."

"No, apparently I've already sold it," she said, with a half-broken laugh. When he frowned, she shook her head. "I'm fine. Really, I am. … It'll just take a few days to figure this out. It's one thing to lose your house and sell it. But it's another thing entirely to realize that I don't even have anything to bother moving. Everything I own is on my back."

She took a deep breath. "I guess, in another way, that's also very freeing. I don't have to worry about packing up or selling things. I don't have to get a moving company." She shook her head. "I can buy it all new at the other end, but I literally have no other end to go to."

"I'll make a suggestion which you probably won't want to hear right now," he offered, with a laugh. "Why not come back to New Mexico with me?"

She turned and stared at him.

"I know it's sudden," he admitted, with a shrug, "but I've gotten used to having you around."

She rolled her eyes and called Thorny over to her. The dog immediately came running.

"Besides, Thorny likes you too."

She nodded. "Just because you've gotten used to rescuing me doesn't mean I need rescuing all the time," she pointed out.

"I wasn't thinking about rescuing you at all," he clarified. "I was thinking about how nice it is to have you in my life. Now, I'm not saying we have to go anywhere with this, and I'm not trying to pressure you into anything more than a destination. I'm just saying that, if you have no other place to go, why not give New Mexico a try? At least you'll have some friends there."

As she sat here in silence, he went on.

"You can't stay here. I mean, you could go to another town. You can go anywhere you want," he told her. "But why not New Mexico?"

She looked at him, and her heart swelled. He was right in the sense that it had been really nice to have him around these last few days. He'd been a huge boon in her world gone crazy. Did she really want to say goodbye to that? No, but, in her mind, she hadn't even thought that saying goodbye would happen.

"It's so weird, and apparently I've gotten so accustomed to having you here," she admitted, "that it hadn't even crossed my mind how you would be leaving soon. Or Thorny," she added, as she crouched to hug the dog.

The War Dog immediately leaned heavily against her, trying to flatten her to the ground. She laughed. "You would think that he would be a little less insistent on sitting on my legs," she muttered, as she struggled to get back up again.

"He just thinks that, if he flattens you down, you won't get up, and he would get more cuddles."

She laughed, giving Thorny as much attention as she could.

"Now, we've got a picnic lunch to eat," Mateo reminded her. "So whereabouts here among these smoldering embers do you want to go? Do you have a place in mind?"

Then she stood up and smiled. "A nice spot is a little farther away." And, with that, she led him to one of her favorite destinations. It wasn't even on her property; it was on public land, with a beautiful river and a park on the side. As they approached, still on foot, she shared, "This is one of my favorite haunts."

"And I can see why," he agreed, with a smile.

"I've spent a lot of time here over the years," she murmured. "Growing up, it was just a place to get away, a place to make decisions, a place to look at the world in a whole different light."

"And it looks to me as if you've made good use of it."

She walked over to the lake and unhooked Thorny. He immediately jumped into the water. She groaned and then shook her head. "Good thing he's your dog."

Mateo stared at her and then started laughing. "Have you forgotten that he's staying in the same motel room as you and me?"

She started to laugh. "I hadn't really considered that," she acknowledged. "I don't think the reality has set in yet."

"I don't think it has either," he agreed, "but the good news is, you have plenty of time."

"I have time," she conceded, "but I don't exactly know that I have any better decision-making ability."

"It doesn't matter." Mateo gave her a wave of his hand. "Take all the time you want. You can come to New Mexico with me, stay at my place—with no pressure—and figure it out as you go."

"Figure it out as I go?" she repeated, with a smile.

"If you don't have any furniture and a bunch of belongings, you can get up and go whenever you want. You won't be beholden to anybody, and you can make decisions all on your own."

"That does sound kind of nice," she noted, "even just getting away. Will I get to meet Badger?"

"Sure. Do you want to meet Badger?"

"Yeah, I need to thank him for sending you, not to mention the rest of it."

"I'm pretty sure that would be Kat, and she would say that she sent me to get Thorny," he corrected, with a chuckle. Moments later, Thorny bounced back out of the water and raced toward them. When they went to grab him and to keep him from going back in, he bounced just out of reach so he could launch himself into the water once more. They played with him for a while until they were all thoroughly soaked.

"Now, I suggest we eat a sandwich and dry off some. Then we can head back to the motel and get into some clean clothes."

"Sounds good." And that's what they did. They sat down and enjoyed their picnic lunch. Thorny stretched out beside them, completely at peace and happy. She watched as Mateo scrubbed his head.

"You really do like dogs, don't you?"

"I do. I like all animals. It's one of those things that is just a part of me. … Just so you know, if you are interested in any kind of relationship with me, I do come with some baggage."

"And the baggage is?"

"Dogs," he declared, with a laugh. "And cats. Well, it could also be an occasional coyote or maybe a squirrel I find. Who knows? I'm really not too fussy. If an animal needs help, I'm right there. I have a friend who is setting up a big refuge not all that far from my place. I might even be involved in building some of the animal pens and stuff with him."

"Seriously?" she asked, staring at him.

"Yeah, he's got all kinds of animals—wildlife, domesticated animals with problems, animals that came from tough situations. You name it, he's got it. He calls it *the Haven*," he shared. "Timber is all heart. It's what he does. It's who he is, and I'm just really happy to be a part of it."

"It sounds like something I would really love to be a part of too," she noted, with a smile.

"You are welcome to join us. Timber's always happy to

have volunteers. It's not a paying position though."

She laughed. "I don't know any sanctuary with a paid position," she declared, with a smile. "Unless, of course, he'll start doing social media and teach about all the animals. In which case, that's a whole different story."

He looked at her and nodded. "You know, you should run that past him."

"I don't know. Maybe. I would have to see. Who knows? What if I don't like any of your friends?"

"It happens," he said. "Can't say I like yours, honestly."

"That's because you haven't met any," she stated, rolling her eyes. "I don't have any here, remember?"

"I'll tell you one thing. You would have lots of friends there."

She stretched out on the grass and felt, for the first time, a sense of peace.

He leaned over and kissed her on the nose. "No pressure, you know?" he repeated.

"I know. I'm in a very different space right now. I would like to have kids one day," she added, looking over at him.

"Good," he replied, with a smile. "Me too. Look at us. We're already getting some of the details out of the way."

She rolled her eyes. "Not really. I just need to know that you're not 100 percent against kids because I do want some at a future point."

"So will I, at some future point," he added, with a smile. "Not necessarily today, not necessarily anytime soon. And listen. I am really sorry about everything you've been through."

"Me too," she whispered, "but again I want to think that bigger, better, and happier times are ahead." She pulled him down and gave him a big kiss, feeling something, feeling almost a sense of homecoming in his arms.

He rolled to the side, pulled her up close, and just held her in the bright sun, letting the world pass by in peaceful and quiet contentment. With Thorny sleeping at her side, she looked up at the bright blue sky and whispered, "It does finally feel as if maybe, just maybe, there's a light in all this."

"There's always a light, but finding it, taking advantage of it, understanding it's even there," he pointed out, "those are all signs of learning to go with the flow and making the best out of things." He leaned over and kissed her again, when suddenly the bark on the tree behind them shattered into small pieces.

MATEO PICKED HER up and tossed her behind the tree, Thorny at her side, barely protected, as Mateo roared, "Stay down and don't move."

She glanced around, trying to figure out what happened, and saw the tree bark all over the ground. "It's them, isn't it?"

"At least one of them." Mateo pulled out his phone and immediately sent off a text message.

"How long before the cavalry gets here?" she asked him.

"I don't know. Depends on where they are and what they're up to, but I can tell you that whoever this is won't wait. If they can, they'll take us out now."

"Jesus, just when I think life will calm down."

"Until the assholes are picked up, it won't really calm down to that level. We always have to make sure that they won't come back after us."

"And that's what this is, isn't it?"

"Yeah. I mean, their whole world has blown up, and they can't continue the life that they had, and, rather than take responsibility for their own choices, they'll just blame you and me."

"That's great," she muttered. "Is that one of the things that's best shared?"

He looked over at her, saw the half-smile on her face, and nodded. "Absolutely. In this case, it's one of the best things shared. You should never be alone when facing this BS."

"That may be true, but it still sucks though."

"Yeah, it still sucks."

Another bullet shattered the trunk, and a man roared, "Get out of hiding, you piece of shit!"

"That's Riley," she stated. "And I can tell you that, when he gets mean like this, it's no holds barred. He will do everything he can to take us out."

"I think I got that message when the tree first exploded," he muttered, as he stared out around the tree. Riley was just barely visible, but Mateo didn't have a weapon. Plus, he had Thorny and Maraya with him, and that meant all bets were off. This Riley guy was playing for keeps, so Mateo had to make sure that playing for keeps didn't go the wrong direction.

He had so much to live for, and he desperately wanted to give Maraya a life that she hadn't yet had, one full of joy, peace, and contentment—instead of forever being on the outs with everyone around her, always being blamed for everything, even though she had had nothing to do with it.

Riley called out again, "Get your sorry ass out here and face me like a man!"

"What good would that do?" Mateo yelled back. "You're

holding a gun. It's not as if you'll face anybody like a man."

He roared, "Don't you say I'm not a man! I'm more man than you'll ever be!"

"I don't think so," Mateo replied, with a sneer. "As far as I'm concerned, you're nothing but a shadow of a man, a shadow of your brother. That's what you are, just a shadow. Too damn bad the good guy died."

After a moment of shocked silence, Riley roared, "You can't fucking talk to me like that!"

"Why not? It's how you talk to everybody else. You hide behind the badge—or the gun. You play little games and make up the rules all on your own. It's not as if you give a shit about anybody."

"Of course I give a shit about people," he yelled. "I give a shit about people who deserve it, not these pieces of shit. Not women like her who can't be bothered to do what they're supposed to do."

"You mean, fall in love with you? You already knew she was basically your brother's wife, the mother of his child. What did you expect? Once your brother was out of the way, did you really think she would just automatically fall in love with you? You aimed too high, Riley. It doesn't work that way," Mateo said into the silence. "Even killing your brother didn't work." More dead silence followed for a long moment, and Mateo peered around the tree to see the rifle facing him and Riley almost vibrating with rage.

"You don't know anything about me, and you don't know anything about my brother. You don't get to talk to me like that."

"Why not?" Mateo asked. "What will you do about it?" Immediately the tree was slammed with bullets, and he recognized just how much of a temper this Riley guy had. A temper completely out of control, but he also hadn't given anything away about killing his brother.

Mateo didn't know whether it was true or not. It was just a shot in the dark to rattle Riley, and it did rattle him—just not enough to readily confess. No point in trying to talk to this guy. That's not what Riley wanted. He wanted his own retribution for whatever had gone wrong in his world, no matter if it was true or not.

As Mateo looked down at Maraya, she had her hand over her mouth, focused on her phone, and he realized she might be recording a video on a live feed again. He wished she wasn't quite so quick to do that, but it had worked in her favor up until now. So, if people saw for themselves that Riley was doing this, it would make the resolution of the mess a whole different story.

Assuming she was broadcasting the feed live, Mateo cried out, "And I see that you don't deny it. Was it worth killing your brother? I mean, you got his job. You got your family's inheritance. You got your family's home. You got everything you could possibly want, including his pregnant girlfriend."

CHAPTER 14

MARAYA COULDN'T BELIEVE Mateo was accusing Riley outright of killing his brother. Admittedly the thought had entered her mind, but she'd never let it stay there long. Yet now, after all that had happened and finding herself in this situation, the more she thought about it, the more she realized just how possible it could be.

She knew there was a chance. "Did you really do that, Riley? How could you kill your own brother? Joseph loved you," she cried out. "Why would you do that to him? Why would you do that to me?"

There was silence for a long moment, and then he asked, "Why not?"

His tone was so conversational and calm, it was eerie … and scary. She stared up at Mateo, her eyes wide. He placed a finger against his lips.

"I mean, it's just all you ever wanted, right?" Mateo asked. "You wanted everything Joseph had. He was always the better brother. The chosen one. Everybody always gave him the credit for everything, but no matter how good you were, nobody cared, right?"

"Nobody ever gave a good goddamn about me," Riley declared, bitterness in his tone. "He was the golden child, the one who got everything."

Mateo put his finger to his lips again, signaling Maraya

to stay silent, hoping to just let Riley talk.

"Our parents even put in their wills that he should have the bulk of the money and the family homestead because he was responsible, and he would look after me. You can bet your sorry ass that he didn't do much looking after me at all. Once the dust settled, he figured all the money was his, and he didn't have to share it at all. But oh no, hell no, I wasn't about to let that happen. I wouldn't let him walk away and take absolutely everything from my life and keep it as his own.

"When that car accident happened, it was as if providence spoke, and I wouldn't say no. I stepped right up to ensure I listened. You can bet Joseph saw the look in my eyes when I stepped into that hospital room too. I told him exactly what I thought of him, and then I held a pillow over his face until he was unconscious. I knocked him off that bed, taking the machinery down with him. It didn't take him long to die. Nobody even thought to look for the cause of death, not after everything in his system was not functioning very well from the accident. They said he would recover, and he would need help breathing for a time, *blah, blah, blah*. You think I gave a shit?"

"So, you killed him, just like that?" Mateo asked.

"It was too easy, the way he went. I didn't want that for him. I wanted him to die, preferably a long and miserable death, at that," he snapped, "but I couldn't take that chance."

Maraya looked on, horrified.

"So, I just did it, to make sure. The torture was nowhere near long enough for me, but I didn't have time to make him suffer any more than that. But you can goddamn bet that he knew. And you, Maraya, you were never supposed to be his girlfriend. You were meant to be mine, but you never even saw me. Once you saw him, you were all over him, just being the whore you are."

She stared in shock, tears coming to her eyes, as she realized how much this man had taken from her, how he had destroyed her world.

"And even then, when you were my wife, do you think you would let me have any peace and quiet? No, you were all about him. Everything was about Joseph. I was so goddamn sick of listening to you spout that bullshit about what a great man he was. He wasn't a great man. He was nothing but a corpse. He wouldn't do anything like share or help me out. No, he was all about himself. I fixed that in the end too," he snapped. "And I don't fucking care. He should have died a whole lot sooner. That would have made my life a whole lot easier."

She was so shocked at what he said. The venom in his words was far beyond anything she had ever contemplated, even in her darkest thoughts. "I had no idea you hated him so much," she called out.

"Of course I hated him. What was there to like? Little Goody Two-Shoes who always could do everything better than anybody else. You know, parents always say they don't have favorites, but that's total bullshit. They have favorites, and everybody else pays. Every single day I paid because Joseph was such a piece of shit. But no, nobody cared about that, as long as he got everything he wanted. Everybody was happy," he said in a mocking tone. "Guess who's happy now?"

"So, you're gonna kill us too now?" Maraya asked.

"Gladly. The best part is that it's not as if you'll do anything about it either," Riley replied. "I'll get out of this just like I've gotten out of everything else I've done over the years. This is my fucking town, and no way you're taking it away from me. You're such a fucking bitch. I can't believe I ever thought I was in love with you."

"You weren't ever in love with me," she called out. "You were obsessed. You made my life miserable for so long, and yet all you could do was keep begging me to come back, begging me to stay with you, begging me to love you," she shared. "I couldn't possibly love you because I was still in love with Joseph. You wanted something from me that I didn't have to give. You always did, even before he died, and I didn't have it to give."

Riley grumbled, "I finally came to that conclusion myself recently, but I figured that—with you gone—my life would be a whole lot easier, and I wouldn't have that constant reminder of failure. It's not as if anybody here would care. They all believe that women have one use and one use only. So, when you're done with them, you ditch them because they weren't worth keeping. I can't say that I did anything to change that attitude, but, hey, it worked in my favor anyway."

She heard his words, but it sounded as if he was getting ever closer. "Just stay away," she cried out.

"Why?" he asked in a mocking tone. "Do you really think I'll let you live after this? You won't go tell anybody about this shit," he declared. "I won't go to jail, not me, not ever.

"I'm tired of hearing about only the good dying young, and listening to everybody else spout off about what a great brother I had. I didn't have a great brother. He was a piece of shit, and I couldn't be happier that he's gone. My parents were pieces of shit too, and everything they did, they did for him. Didn't matter who else was involved, it was all about Joseph. I'm so goddamn sick of listening to that shit," he roared.

"You don't have to now," she yelled back. "They're all dead."

"But not you," he said, with a laugh. "I don't think I'll be happy until you're gone too. I thought I could let you go. I thought I could let you go off and do your own merry thing, and I wouldn't give a shit. And you're right. I don't give a shit, except that every time I see you, I see *him*, and that is something I will not let stand. Sorry, but not sorry, you'll be the next casualty, and nobody will fucking care."

She held her tongue, letting him incriminate himself so at least the truth would finally be out there, no matter how this ended.

Riley continued on. "How does that feel? How does it feel to know everybody in this town is against you? I made sure of that. I told them all kinds of tales about how bad you were, and terrible things you probably would have told me if you'd had the guts. That's why they think you're the worse person in the world and why all of them hate you. Getting you sectioned for no reason was just sheer fun. For all these years, they've talked behind your back and repeated horrible things about you. Most of the time you didn't even know." Riley chuckled. "I poisoned every good memory you could possibly have because, if you wouldn't love me, I would ensure nobody could possibly love you either."

A sound came from left, and she really wanted him to stay where he was, but Riley crept closer and closer. She pulled frantically at Mateo's leg, and he looked down at her and placed a finger against her lip and then pointed. She realized he had sent Thorny off to the side of the brush, just out of sight. She saw the War Dog, but no way Riley could see him from his position.

She stared at the dog, not sure what would happen, worrying that Thorny might die, yet, as far as Mateo was concerned, this was a good thing. She didn't see it herself, but, if he was confident, at least it gave her a moment to catch her breath and to try to talk to Riley some more. "Riley, if you shoot us, it'll just make things worse for you."

"No way. It will make things better, much better, and I'll be happier," he explained, with a smile. "It won't be worse at all. It's definitely time that you met your maker."

Mateo motioned her to keep Riley talking. "What then, repenting of my sins and all?"

"Something like that. I should have done it a long time ago, and I've always regretted not doing it when you miscarried. That would have been perfect. Hell, I could have just made you bleed out, and it would have been fine. Nobody would have given it a second thought. As it was, that was the luckiest thing ever. No way I would have my brother's brat running around, so that saved me a lot of trouble. Good job losing the kid."

She closed her eyes against the wave of pain brought by the memory of that loss and the shock even now at Riley's cruelty. She'd been so devastated and overwrought with grief, both for her baby and for her last connection to Joseph. Yet to hear the way Riley spoke about it, so casual and cruel, it was enough to break her heart all over again. It was all she could do to stifle the sobs as memories overwhelmed her.

"You couldn't have thought I would allow another guy around you," he roared. "No fucking way. That just won't happen. Besides, you'll always just be constantly thinking about my brother. I'm doing this guy a favor because it would be a living nightmare for him. So it's best all around that neither of you gets to live that long," he declared, with a reckless laugh.

"What about your deputies? What about all the damage they did?"

"So, they burned down your house. It was pretty stupid on their part, but they were just trying to make me happy, to please me. Those two are always trying to one-up each other, trying to be my favorite," he explained. "It's an interesting system for generating employee loyalty."

"That's not loyalty," she yelled. "That's abuse in its own right. You encouraged them to be bullies and bigots. But where was the line? Where would it stop? How many others have you turned them loose on?"

"Oh, good Christ, save me from your bleeding heart. All that talk about abuse. Jesus, haven't you figured out that nobody gives a shit? Abuse is just what you can dish out and not have to pay for," Riley explained. "Rodney and Xavier are just plain stupid and don't have a full brain between them, if you ask me. But they're my deputies, and they do my bidding. So, believe me that I'll keep them around for that reason alone."

She rolled her eyes and continued. "Yet, you aren't keeping them around because they're in deep trouble now."

"Yeah, and whose fault is that?" he snapped. "Who the hell would want to have anything to do with you in any way, shape, or form when you're such a walking, talking mess?" he declared in disgust. "You're a complete shitshow, and you just go around destroying things for everybody else."

"You're a fine one to talk. Killing your brother, burning houses, leaving children to suffer in the woods, and you blame me?"

"I do blame you—for all of it. I can't believe that you got my deputies in trouble. And now they're both on the run because of you. Do you have any idea what it'll take for me to calm this all down again and get everybody back on our side and agreeing my guys were forced into running because they thought you had all these people lined on your side, how nobody would listen to the good local citizens?"

"You'll have to pull out all the stops to get anybody to believe that."

"Yeah, but I will. I'll make it work. Jesus, what a fucking pain in the ass you are."

As she sat here, she realized he probably could make it work. After years of listening to him tell lies about her, he probably could make it work. Everybody was more or less willing to believe everything he said. Even now, they probably wouldn't understand the reality and would go for the status quo because it required no effort to think on their part. She closed her eyes and asked, "So, what are you expecting now, Riley?"

"I'm not expecting anything. I'll just make it a murder-suicide."

"How do you plan to pull that off?" she asked.

"You'll kill this guy, and then you'll kill yourself."

She looked up at Mateo in shock, as he stared at her grimly. She realized that Riley had envisioned a scenario that the entire town would believe. Immediately she hopped to her feet, but Mateo grabbed her and pulled her back so she was still hidden. "He'll get away with it," she whispered, staring at Mateo.

"Only if he shoots us," he pointed out. "Remember that he has to kill us first."

She swallowed hard and nodded. "I hope you've got a

plan up your sleeve," she whispered, "because I don't have anything."

He just smiled and called back to Riley, "Why don't you come over here and talk to us?"

"I'd love to," he snapped.

"Of course, you'll have to leave the gun where you are."

"Nope, not happening," he said. "I like having the upper hand."

"You've always had the upper hand. That's what you do, isn't it? I mean, it's not as if you ever give people a fair shake. You're only happy as long as you're getting what you consider to be the better deal."

"That's because I spent a lifetime getting the shaft," he declared, followed by a dry laugh. "But not now. Nobody treats me like that now."

"Sorry about your brother," she said. "I had no idea."

"Nobody did. Everybody just saw the angel, but he was a real piece of shit."

She had to wonder if she had only seen one side of him too. Was everything Riley said possible? Of course, it was possible, but was it probable? She hadn't really begun to figure it out when she heard footsteps coming toward her, sounding a lot closer. She closed her eyes and said, "Please don't do this."

"Of course I'll do it," Riley declared, with a laugh. "No freaking way I'm backing out now."

Just then shouts came from the road above.

Riley turned, looked, and then raced toward Mateo and Maraya, as if in a last-ditch effort to take them out. "What the hell did you do, you stupid bitch?" he roared.

"For one thing, I've been streaming this live on social media," she replied, holding up her phone and tracking him right on the video.

He stared at her in shock.

"So, even if you do kill us," she added, "at least you won't get away with it."

"Oh no, no, no," he yelled. "That's not happening."

He raised his gun just as she was dragged back behind the tree. The tree was immediately splattered with bullets again, only to be followed by a high-pitched scream.

She peered around the tree—fighting against Mateo, still holding her back—to see Thorny chomping down hard on Riley's wrist. Immediately Mateo let her go, so he could knock Riley to the ground, flipping him over and pinning him down, before Mateo called off Thorny.

She walked up slowly as the gun was kicked away, and she kicked it even farther. She glanced down at Mateo and asked, "What the hell was that?"

Mateo smiled. "I imagine the guys just got here."

And, sure enough, within seconds, Jacks and Jacob broke through the trees and raced toward them. They stopped, looked down at the sheriff.

Jacob muttered, "Hell, we're late again."

Jacks looked back at Mateo and added, "Pretty good timing you've got, buddy."

"I was hoping that you would get here a little sooner, but we got a lot of it recorded anyway."

"Lots of audio and even some video there at the end," she added, holding up her phone.

The two men smiled at her. "I'm not sure about hanging out around you. I mean, if you'll record everything on social media, that's not our thing," Jacks teased.

"It's not mine either," she stated, "but, when you've got nothing else as a weapon, you use whatever you can."

"Agreed."

They reached down and quickly put restraints on Riley's wrists and pulled him to his feet.

He was sputtering in fury at her. "It won't stop," he snapped. "No way anybody'll believe that."

"It's all in your own words, Riley," she pointed out. "We'll let the people decide what they want to believe." As Jacks and Jacob carted off Riley, she turned to Mateo. "New Mexico sounds like a damn fine destination."

"Really?" he asked, with a big grin.

"Yeah," she said. "I'm thinking the air down there smells a whole lot better than here."

And, with a last glance at Riley and at the world she had lived in for so long, she turned her back on her ex and headed to her car.

CHAPTER 15

SEVERAL DAYS AND one long road trip later, Mateo and Maraya pulled up in front of Mateo's house. "This is home," he announced, with a smile. He watched as her eyes widened at the huge plantation-style home in front of her, and she was immediately at a loss for words.

"Holy crap, this is gorgeous," she muttered, when she could finally speak.

"Land in this particular area is a whole lot cheaper, and we certainly can buy a lot more for the dollar. But this is my kind of home," he stated, with pride.

"It's gorgeous. Absolutely gorgeous." And then she noted several dogs were in the yard and other animals were around the corner. "Are you sure that friend of yours has the animal refuge? It looks to me as if you have plenty of animals yourself."

"I'll always have animals," he stated. "Remember?"

"Oh, I remember. It was one of the conditions you set to having a relationship as I recall," she teased.

He frowned. "Sounds arrogant when you say it that way. Sorry."

"No, I can appreciate ground rules."

"Oh, that's definitely true," he agreed, with a smile. He hopped out, and she followed, a little bit slower, as she watched Thorny race out behind him and head toward the front yard, where he was sniffing the other dogs over the top of the fence. "Will Thorny be okay here with the other dogs?"

"Yep, he'll be just fine. It will take him a day or two to acclimate, but I think all the dogs will work it out and will get along just fine."

She watched with a smile on her face as Mateo let the dogs introduce themselves to each other. Then he opened the gate so they could really meet.

Immediately they surrounded each other, sniffing and tails wagging all around, and she smiled. "You know, if life was always this easy, it would be so much simpler."

"Wouldn't it?" he said with a smile, as he motioned at the house. "Welcome to my place."

"And do we get to spend a few days here, or do you have to go to work with Badger all the time?"

"I won't be working today and probably not tomorrow," he shared, with an eye roll, "but I can't guarantee that. I'm really hoping we'll have a couple days together to chill out a bit."

"I feel as if you haven't really had any time off as it is," she pointed out. "I mean, look at all the stuff you've been doing just to help get me back to work again."

"Not just about work even," he clarified. "Just getting you here was plenty, between getting the sales paperwork done, reading over all the arson reports, and of course we had to deal with the interviews, plus the lawyers, and all those prosecutors. Some of that will be ongoing, but, in the meantime, you have a whole new place to call home."

He grabbed their bags and carried them up to the house, her following behind him. "This is absolutely amazing."

"It is, isn't it? The bedrooms are up here." He walked

into the master, dropped her bag, and announced, "You can have this room. You've got an en suite bathroom and lots of space here. You can spend some time and figure out what you really want to do with your life, and go from there." He pointed beyond this room. "I'll be right next door if you need me."

"That sounds good to me," she whispered, as she stared around the absolutely massive room with sunlight beaming in one window, casting beautiful shadows across the entire room. "I can't believe this is your place. It's beautiful."

He nodded. "I'm really happy with it. … This was my relocation and my attempt at a whole new life. And, if I did it, you can do it too."

She laughed. "I wasn't thinking about that, but I will admit you do make it pretty easy when you offer all this help."

"Hey, you've still got insurance to deal with, and plenty of other stuff, but considering where you were, and what you've just gone through, life now is probably looking pretty good. I personally wouldn't be too upset at where you're sitting right now."

"I'm not upset at all," she declared, giving him a bright smile. "This is pretty-damn nice." Looking out the window, she watched the dogs running around all over the place. Laughing, she added, "It'll be a little crazy though."

"Hey, I've only got four dogs right now. I do foster quite a few and give Timber a hand when I need to," he added, with a shrug. "The guys do too. I'm assuming they are home already, since they left before us."

"So, we'll see Jacob and Jacks here too?" she asked, surprised. "I didn't realize they lived here."

"Yeah, they're close by. Everybody is involved in Badger's construction projects, one way or another," he said, with a huge smile. "So, as long as you don't mind being part of a community, there's definitely room for you here."

"I don't mind in the least," she stated warmly. "It'll be nice to feel welcome somewhere."

"You won't have to worry about that here," he said, giving her a hug. "Everybody can't wait to meet you."

"And when will that be?" she asked.

"Not for a few days." He laughed, seeing her nervous smile. "I told them not to push it, and we would get there when we get there."

"Thank you," she said immediately. "It's nice to know I'll have a little time to get settled."

"A little bit but not a ton," he noted, with a laugh. "Everybody is pretty anxious to have you come by."

From the look on her face, she hadn't been expecting that kind of a welcome. As he walked out of the room, he asked, "What do you want to do now? Go for a walk, have a shower, chill? What's your pleasure, ma'am?"

She stopped at the door, leaned against it, and smiled up at him. "Seriously?"

"Yeah. Wait. What do you mean?" he asked, clearly confused.

She frowned. "You've put me in a bedroom. You've got your house all set up and organized the way you like it, and now it's all about what I want to do?" she asked, shaking her head.

"I don't get it." Mateo frowned. "Did I do something wrong?"

She burst out laughing. "I haven't had a welcome kiss or anything," she teased. "I could use one of those."

He immediately snagged her up into his arms and laid a

kiss on her that she wouldn't soon forget. "There's that one," he murmured against her hair. "Or there's this one." And he lowered his head again.

This time a sultry heat filled her heart and soul as he gave her a true welcome kiss of the likes that made her toes curl. She opened her eyes and stared up at him. "Good God," she whispered, sliding her arms around his neck. "If I'd realized you were hiding that, I would have brought it up a lot earlier."

"It's not exactly been hiding. It's just something I was trying to be good about."

"Skip the *being good* part," she said, wrapping her arms around him, standing on her tiptoes, and giving him a hard kiss of her own. "Because, honest to God, I'm more than happy to spend the rest of the afternoon lying on the bed in that ray of sunshine, just spending time with you," she shared.

"I figured," he said cockily.

She laughed. "I don't really want to meet everybody just yet. Maybe in a day or two when I'm a little more comfortable," she added, "but I would really love to spend some time just as us. That would be good for now."

He lowered his head once more and stopped short of her lips. "I was trying not to get too pushy or to pressure you. I wanted to give you time to figure out what you wanted to do," he murmured, as he kissed her on the cheek and then kissed her on the chin and then again on her nose. "You've been through an awful lot. I didn't want you to feel—"

With that, she plastered a kiss on his lips as if she were a drowning woman and he her lifeline. When she lifted her head this time, he was breathing hard and fast.

He stared down at her, his heart slamming against his

chest. "Okay, but that'll lead you directly to one place," he declared.

"Thank goodness for that." Bursting into laughter, she stepped out of his hands, and headed toward the bed, chucking off her clothing as she went. "Otherwise"—she turned to look back at him—"I just might have to get mean."

He grinned. "And what will that be like? No offense, but it sounds like a threat from a little butterfly." With a gasp, she opened her eyes wide and glared at him. He burst out laughing. "Sweetheart, you can come and get me anytime you want."

"I could not," she declared immediately. "It's not who I am."

"I know, and that's why it was an easy thing to tell you," he said, with a big grin. "On the other hand, any time you want to spend an afternoon in bed, just getting to know each other"—he waggled his eyebrows—"I'm definitely your guy."

"I only have one guy," she declared, with a smirk, "and he's right here in front of me." She wrapped her arms around him and tugged him onto the bed. "But I will say you are a little overdressed."

"Somebody put me on the bed," he noted, stretching out. "So, you might just have to help."

"*Ooh.*" She waggled her eyebrows. "I think I can handle that." And she immediately put her hands on his belt buckle and felt his body react instantly. She laughed out loud. "Glad to know everything is functioning."

"Oh, I would say so," he muttered, then gasping as she slid a hand into his jeans, where she cupped him. He swore, his hands immediately releasing his belt as she hadn't bothered with any of the basics. He shoved off his jeans and pulled his T-shirt over his head. Before she knew it, he was down to just socks.

As he went to take them off, she flipped him backward onto the bed and said, "I kind of like them." She immediately straddled his hips and sat down on top of his erection, holding it tight between the two of them. He sucked in his breath and shuddered. She leaned over and cuddled him and whispered, "I've been waiting for this since I first met you." His eyes opened wide, and she nodded. "You were gorgeous to me even then," she admitted. "Yet my life was such a freaking mess. I didn't have a clue what I was doing, and I didn't want to add to the drama."

"And I didn't want to add to your stress and confusion either," he whispered, as he drew a finger from her chin down between her breasts to her belly button and her hip bone. Then he started massaging and stroking her skin up to her chest and across, cupping her breasts, weighing them in his hands, sighing with pleasure at their softness and resilience, just the joy of being with her in this moment. "You're beautiful, you know?" he asked. "Inside and out."

"Oh no," she said. "You don't get to fob me off with compliments."

"Oh really?" he asked, with a chuckle. "Because I fully intend to completely overwhelm you with compliments, from now until there is no *us* anymore."

She immediately placed a finger on his lips. "That's not happening. When I go into a relationship," she stated, "I go into it with all my heart."

"And what about Riley?"

"That wasn't a relationship. I'm not even sure how I ended up married to him in the first place," she whispered, accompanied by a shudder. "It wasn't me. It wasn't my choice, and maybe it was just this pathetic young woman who needed to know she was safe. I don't know what that was," she admitted, "but I was overwhelmed, definitely not who I am today. Going into a relationship isn't an easy thing for me," she added, staring intently at Mateo. "It takes a lot of trust, and yet I don't have any hesitation about going in that direction with you, and that says a lot."

"It does," he agreed, as he pulled her down closer. "And I promise I won't ever break that trust."

"And you know something? I believe you, and I wouldn't have thought that was possible," she replied, as she kissed his jaw. "You have shown me such a different side of people, of men, and that's truly been a blessing to have you in my life," she whispered, as she leaned over and kissed him again, her breasts brushing against his chest.

He groaned softly and shifted his hips, pushing up tighter against her mound, and whispered, "You know, we could just stop talking for a while."

"We could," she said, as she let her tongue drift across his chin and his lips, tasting, exploring, all on her own. "But I don't want this over too fast."

"Oh, but we could have it over fast, and then we could do it again," he suggested, waggling his eyebrows, "when it's not such a pressure-cooker."

She burst out laughing at that. "Don't tell me that you don't have enough control," she said, as she wiggled on top of his erection.

He shuddered again and moaned. "If you keep that up, it'll be over very quickly, and that would be a shame."

"It might be a shame," she agreed, "but it could be interesting if we work out some of that urgency and then turn around for a second go."

"In that case—" He quickly flipped her onto her back, and she burst out laughing, only to have the laughter stilled as his lips crushed hers, as he shifted his position so that he was at the entrance to the heart of her.

She shuddered, feeling him pulse right there against her. She opened her thighs wide, wrapped them around his hips, and whispered, "Now, damn it. Do it now."

But he held back and gently stroked her, raising her need to the point that she couldn't do anything but cry out at his ministrations. Finally he surged deep inside her and stilled. She froze, slowly adjusting, getting used to having him there, filling her to the point that she didn't think she could handle anything else. Finally she settled back, and he whispered, "Are you okay?"

She nodded. "Never better."

And, with that, he started to move. Slowly at first, then faster and faster, until she exploded in his arms, her body arching up beneath him, only to hold him close as he found his own release and then collapsed beside her.

She groaned against his lips and whispered, "Did you say round two?"

He burst out laughing and nodded. "Yes, but I'll need a couple minutes."

"Okay, I'm counting."

He looked up to see if she was serious, but she flashed him a big grin. With that, he rolled her over, pulled her up tight, and held her close. "We will enjoy our life together," he whispered. "There's really just laughter and love and joy in our world, lots of it."

"Good," she murmured. "I could use some of all that."

"I promise we'll have a life full of laughter and love and

joy. When you least expect it, you'll look over and see me, and you'll smile because it's a life you never thought you would have," he whispered. "And I promise you will never regret it."

"I could never regret this," she whispered, as she looked up at him. "It brought me here, to this moment with you, and that is perfect for me."

He pulled her up tighter and asked, "Are you sure you don't want to nap for a bit?"

She pushed him back. "Hell no, I want round two."

And they proceeded to start all over again.

EPILOGUE

B ADGER LEANED AGAINST the doorjamb and crossed his arms. Then he shifted ever-so-slightly to a more comfortable position as he studied his wife, organizing files on the large table. The *boardroom table*, they mockingly called it, but it ended up being a greet-all, meet-all, do-all-kinds-of-stuff table. He never expected them to ever need this, but, now that they had it, he couldn't imagine doing without it.

Kat looked up, smiled, and then returned to the paper-work in front of her.

Only as Badger saw *K9* on one of sheets of paper did his eyebrows shoot up. "More?" he asked in surprise.

She smirked, tilted her head at him, and nodded. "Just a few."

He snorted at that. "What do you mean, just a few?" Then he dropped his arms, stepped closer, and added, "I thought Timber would be handling these."

"Well, maybe when Timber's life calms down and when he has a chance to look up from the chaos of his world so he can even *see* what needs to be done, then maybe he will," she explained, with a nod. "In the meantime, you and I both know he has his hands full."

Not much Badger could say about that since Timber was caught up in the roaring success of his animal sanctuary so far. Yet the ongoing construction was endless, the needs of the animals endless, the needs of the people volunteering to help also endless. Badger imagined that checking on one of these War Dog cases would probably be out of the scope of what Timber could do right now.

"How is it that we were so sure he could take them on down the road?" she wondered, out loud.

"Not sure. Regardless," he said, as he looked at the number of files on the desk, "this is more than a *few* files." He couldn't see each one as they were thin and tightly stacked together now.

"I know it's a lot to handle for one person, but it was always the plan that, at some point, Timber could take over what I'm doing," she said, looking up at him, yet with a bright smile.

"Doing what exactly?" he asked, teasing her.

"Finding people to deal with these cases. But better yet—"

He nodded and interrupted, "Better yet that War Dogs stop going missing—or that their owners stop going missing—and that the government close those gaps in this entire routine. That way, we don't end up with all these cases." He noted she was holding one, clutched in her hands. He sighed and asked, "And who is it you are pulling off my team for this now?"

She chuckled. "It's not that I'm pulling out anybody, but you do have a bunch of new people."

"Yeah, I had to bring in new recruits," he muttered, shaking his head. "So many of the guys we were working with headed up to Timber's place and now have decided to stay there permanently."

"Well, if they went there, and that's where they are

needed, then that's where they belong," she stated firmly.

"I know. I do understand," Badger acknowledged. "It's just handy when we have men to cover all the trades right here. It's a nuisance when we're missing a few, ... like right now."

She shrugged. "Oh, come on. A couple plumbers will be back from Timber's place soon enough."

"I know," he conceded, "but I could really use another electrician right now too."

She nodded. "Well, this guy is a welder, or he *was* a welder anyway." She frowned as she glanced down at the paperwork in her hand. "He also was a field medic for a while." Kat smiled at her husband and added, "He's a highly certified mechanic."

"Great," Badger said excitedly. "You know that we always need them."

She laughed and laughed. "Maybe, and maybe they need something other than us, even if just for a few days."

He nodded, his good cheer falling away. "I get it," he muttered. "So, who is it that you're planning on pulling out of here now?"

She smiled. "Wilden."

Badger's eyebrows shot up. "Wilden Hookman?"

"Yes," she confirmed, with a sideways glance in his direction. He frowned at her as she nodded. "I know that he's been a big help for you."

"It's not only that I have a lot of use for him," he protested, "but I'm not sure he's ready for too much excitement. He's here because he wants peace and quiet," he pointed out. "Just because you think he might be perfect for this case doesn't mean he's ready for all it may entail."

"True," she admitted, her smile broad and understanding, "and you will always take their side if you think it's something they need to be protected from."

He shuffled a little uneasily, and then stepped forward, grabbed the closest chair, and sat down. "I'm not trying to protect them," he grumbled.

"Yes, you are," she said gently, "and I understand. You see them for who they are, but I see them for who they can be."

He stopped and stared, then frowned. "Somehow your version of the story always sounds better than mine," he muttered, "and I'm not sure how I got on the opposite side of this."

"There is no opposite side," she declared, with a pat of his hand. "Just the way I'm looking to always improve their prosthetics and to see how to maximize what they can do, you see them at the broken, wounded stage of who they are now, needing that hideaway spot, needing a place, a safe haven."

"Well, that's Timber's domain now," he muttered.

"And ours in many ways," she added. "We have helped these guys get back on their feet, and we'll continue to do that. As you well know, it's not *one and done* by any means."

He shifted, thinking it over, because she was right. "In this case, I would say that Wilden is quite possibly ready to do something more and that this could be a good option. Will he want to? I don't know."

"I really hope he does because it'll also involve his family."

"Ah," Badger muttered, now understanding. "That's why you chose him."

"To a certain extent, yes, that's why I chose him," she confirmed, with a chuckle.

"So, maybe you need to bring him in and ask him if he's even interested."

"Interested in what?" a man asked.

A deep booming voice behind Badger made him start and turn toward the doorway. Wilden, tall and blond, stood in the doorway, his hair pushed back as if he'd been running his fingers through it in frustration, or maybe in an attempt to control it, or just to enjoy being out in the wind.

Badger invited him to sit and filled him in.

Wilden sat here for few moments, his face devoid of any emotional expressions or any indication of how he felt about this proposal.

"So, what do you think?" Badger asked Wilden.

"She did mention it to me," he said cautiously, pointing to Kat, "but I hadn't spoken to you about it because I didn't think it was imminent."

Badger nodded and said, "Believe me, if my wife has spoken to you about almost anything, it's as good as gold, and you should consider it imminent."

Wilden shrugged. "Not that it's a done deal," he began, "but, because of what Kat mentioned, it feels as if I need to go home anyway."

Kat asked him, "Did you think about my offer or do you just want to go home and not even consider the work for us?"

"Well, the missing War Dog does give me a reasonable excuse to go home," he replied, "but I should be going home for my grandmother."

"Your grandmother?" Badger asked.

"Yeah, she's the only family I have left," he shared. "So, if I can do something to help her, I will."

Badger frowned. "And yet you've had the time and the

chance to do this earlier, but you haven't gone home before?"

"No," he said, "because my father was still alive. According to Kat, he apparently passed away in the last couple weeks."

"You didn't know?" Badger asked, staring at him.

"I didn't know about it because nobody told me," Wilden explained, with a pensive look.

"You don't talk to anyone back home?" Badger asked.

"Not recently," he said, shaking his head. "So, I'm preparing to go home, I guess." He hesitated and asked, "As long as you don't have a problem with that?"

Badger immediately waved that off. "If you need to go home, you go home. Anything happening here is neither here nor there, as far as I'm concerned. Family comes first."

Wilden smiled and said, "I was hoping you would be okay with it."

"Absolutely. And is your grandmother likely to welcome you with open arms?"

"She would have at one time," he noted, with a dry laugh. "My father made a point of making sure nothing was there for me and kept himself squarely between her and me. So, I don't know what I'll find when I get back there." He looked over at Kat and asked, "Did you get the file on the dog?"

"I have it here," she said, as she dropped it on the table in front of him. "This is all we have."

He opened it up, and, even as he read through it, he shot her a look.

She nodded and grimaced. "Sorry. That's usually all we end up with, one single page. In this case, the dog's name is Sarge, and he was given to a veteran who had worked with dogs a lot during his own time in the military. As far as we knew, he and the dog were fine."

"What happened?"

"The dog was found loose, running around town. When he was scanned, the microchip triggered an alert. Apparently the adoptee has disappeared, and nobody knows anything about where he went. The dog is currently waiting at the clinic, but they are having a lot of trouble getting him to stay."

"As in?"

"He's trying to escape his cage, and they feel very strongly that he's trying to help his owner, but only one person works there, and she doesn't have anybody to give her a hand. She's also just lost one of her partners."

"*Lost*, as in?"

"Her partner in the practice has moved away, leaving her alone to run a practice meant for three working vets. So she is overwhelmed and has no time to go looking for the missing man. She's keeping the dog safe, but his behavior means keeping him locked up."

Wilden frowned. "That could be for a lot of reasons."

"Absolutely it could be." She shrugged. "The bottom line is that somebody needs to figure out what's going on, and Sarge needs some home care."

"Any specific reason for that?"

"Yeah," she said, with a nod. "He was injured, but I didn't get a report from her as to what the injuries were."

"Not enough to stop him from trying to escape apparently," Wilden noted, with a smile.

"And we do know that a lot of animals will forget their own injuries in order to help others."

"Exactly," he said. "How long has this been going on?"

"A couple days," she said.

"So, it hasn't been very long. What about the owner?"

"We have no police report. I don't have anything on him except that a wellness check was done at his place at my behest, and there's no sign of him, though it sounded like the place has been tossed. But they don't consider it a missing person's case because he's an adult and hasn't been gone all that long." Then she sighed and shrugged. "If you knew how many times we've been told that story because the local authorities don't want to be bothered," she noted, "it would make your heart sick."

"Oh, I get it," he said. "I've seen it time and time again." He looked over at her. "What's the name of the old guy?"

"Jackson Russell," she said.

His eyebrows shot up. "Jackson Russell? Jeez, he's got to be close to my grandmother's age." Then he frowned and thought about it for a moment. "No, I guess he would probably be a generation younger. But they were friends, way back when. How soon can I get there?" He stood, ready to leave.

"You're leaving tonight, if you're okay with it."

"I'm definitely okay with it," he agreed, turning, almost stumbling, and now swearing.

Kat called out to him, "Take it easy on that leg, and, when you come back, we'll get that new prototype set up."

He turned to her and asked, "Is that something you do for everybody who goes after your missing War Dogs?"

"It's something I try to do for everybody," she clarified. "Yet, if you'll put it through some rough days, you'll need an upgrade. I don't have anything here and ready for you now, but, if you go after this dog, we'll see what you need when you get back. You take good care of yourself."

He nodded. "Sometimes shit happens, doesn't it?"

"Shit always happens," Badger noted. "It's how you handle it that makes all the difference. Whether you've got a teaspoon or a shovel," he added, "it's up to you to make the best of it."

And, with that, Wilden shot him a hard look. "I'm okay to make the best of it," he said, "but sometimes there's just no making anything else out of something like this." And, with that, he turned and walked out.

Badger looked over at Kat, who just shrugged and explained, "My understanding is a major dispute came up between father and son way back when. Although Wilden was raised by his grandmother, some issues have since appeared."

"Probably to do with the military," he suggested.

"That's very possible," she murmured. "And, now that his father has passed, Wilden's willing to go back, and this War Dog case will give him a chance to deal with his family issues. If we're lucky, we can help a veteran and his dog."

Badger studied his wife and smiled. "Wow, you're just aiming higher every time, aren't you?"

She chuckled. "In this case, I think it's warranted."

This concludes Book 30 of The K9 Files: Mateo.
Read about Wilden: The K9 Files, Book 31

The K9 Files: Wilden (Book #31)

Welcome to the all new K9 Files series reconnecting readers with the unforgettable men from SEALs of Steel in a new series of action packed, page turning romantic suspense that fans have come to expect from USA TODAY Bestselling author Dale Mayer. Pssst... you'll meet other favorite characters from SEALs of Honor and Heroes for Hire too!

Wilden was eager to return to his grandmother's side, now that his father was gone. She had sent him away for his safety, and he had stayed away. Yet what awaited him was far from what he had imagined. Retrieving the War Dog from the animal clinic and the mystery of its missing veteran owner just added to the intrigue.

Vivian had reached out to Kat, the expert on War Dog issues, never anticipating how one phone call would alter her life forever. The agitated dog was just the beginning.

Discovering Vivian with Sarge was a relief for Wilden, but it also brought a whirlwind of questions about his father's death and the missing War Dog's owner. Wilden was determined to uncover the truth. With Vivian by his side, Wilden didn't foresee the storm of animosity that would challenge their growing bond—or their very lives …

Find Book 31 here!
To find out more visit Dale Mayer's website.
https://geni.us/DMSWilden

Author's Note

Thank you for reading Mateo: The K9 Files, Book 30! If you enjoyed the book, please take a moment and leave a short review.

Dear reader,

I love to hear from readers, and you can contact me at my website: www.dalemayer.com or at my Facebook author page. To be informed of new releases and special offers, sign up for my newsletter or follow me on BookBub. And if you are interested in joining Dale Mayer's Reader Group, here is the Facebook sign up page.
http://geni.us/DaleMayerFBGroup

Cheers,
Dale Mayer

About the Author

Dale Mayer is a *USA Today* best-selling author, best known for her SEALs military romances, her Psychic Visions series, and her Lovely Lethal Garden cozy series. Her contemporary romances are raw and full of passion and emotion (Broken But … Mending, Hathaway House series). Her thrillers will keep you guessing (Kate Morgan, By Death series), and her romantic comedies will keep you giggling (*It's a Dog's Life*, a stand-alone novella; and the Broken Protocols series, starring Charming Marvin, the cat).

Dale honors the stories that come to her—and some of them are crazy, break all the rules and cross multiple genres!

To go with her fiction, she also writes nonfiction in many different fields, with books available on résumé writing, companion gardening, and the US mortgage system. All her books are available in print and ebook format.

Connect with Dale Mayer Online

Dale's Website – www.dalemayer.com
Twitter – @DaleMayer
Facebook Page – geni.us/DaleMayerFBFanPage
Facebook Group – geni.us/DaleMayerFBGroup
BookBub – geni.us/DaleMayerBookbub
Instagram – geni.us/DaleMayerInstagram
Goodreads – geni.us/DaleMayerGoodreads
Newsletter – geni.us/DaleNews